WAITING FOR MURDER

FLEUR HITCHCOCK

nosy
crow

First published in the UK in 2021 by Nosy Crow Ltd
The Crow's Nest, 14 Baden Place
Crosby Row, London, SE1 1YW

www.nosycrow.com

ISBN: 978 1 78800 864 8

A CIP catalogue record for this book is available from the British Library.

Printed and bound in Great Britain by Clays Ltd, Elcograf S.p.A.
Typeset by Tiger Media

Papers used by Nosy Crow are made from
wood grown in sustainable forests.

MIX
Paper from
responsible sources
FSC® C018072

1 3 5 7 9 10 8 6 4 2

Prologue

They were draining the Sandford reservoir. Small things were emerging from the mud and baking in the heat, but I didn't see the roof of the car until three days into our stay.

By the fourth day the top of the window was showing.

By then I could see that there was something, or someone, inside.

Chapter I

I'm being watched.

But I'm going to pretend that I don't know it.

I'm lying on the baked grass staring up through the leaves of an enormous tree. Small things are crawling over my ankles. I can feel them but it's too hot to move. Mum's sitting on a blanket next to me; beyond her are David and Anya, the two other archaeologists. It's so hot they've stopped talking. Even the pigeons have given up. The only sound is a generator and a softer drone, a summer hum of bees and crickets. Every now and again a hot breeze rattles the dry grass and the leaves rustle overhead.

"Have some coleslaw, Dan." Mum shoves a small plastic box my way. It's encrusted with congealed mayonnaise.

Pushing it back towards her, I roll on to my stomach to look across the lake. To my left is the dam. A group of people are standing on the top, staring down into the green soupy water of the emptying reservoir. Some of them are wearing hard hats and high-vis jackets. They must be very hot. Every now and then they tap the huge pipes that are pumping the water out of the lake into the fields behind and say things to one another and rub their chins. I'm not sure what they're going to achieve by looking at the water. It's so thick with weed and algae that it doesn't even make me feel cooler.

Further round to the right is a line of trees.

Below them is a girl sitting in the shade of a tree. I don't think she knows she can be seen. I think she thinks she's hidden. She's got her knees bunched up in front of her and she's peering across the lake with binoculars.

I wave and she drops the binoculars.

I knew I was being watched.

I roll over again and sit up, resting my chin on my knees so that I can stare at her across the lake.

"Who's that, Dan?" asks Mum.

"Dunno."

"Go and say hello," she says.

"Mum," I moan. "I'm not four."

She waves her hand at me. "Too hot to argue – s'just if we're here for weeks, you're going to need someone to talk to."

It's getting cooler now. It still feels epically hot but I can move out of the shade without fainting. The birds seem to have woken up and they're swooping over the lake eating insects. Mum and the other archaeologists are back under their white gazebo scratching at the dirt. They're looking for the grave of a woman called Edith the Fair. She died about a thousand years ago and no one knows where she ended up, but when they started to drain the lake, someone found a gravestone and some bones, and Mum, who's a bone expert, plucked me out of my happy city summer and brought me here. I'm sure she'd be thrilled if she found a gold necklace or something, but she gets just as excited by a skeleton, and she seems to be able to find out all kinds of stuff about bones just from looking at them. It's a sort of superpower. A bone one.

Across the reservoir, the girl with the binoculars is talking to someone. It's another girl, this one lying on her back looking at her phone. Tracing an imaginary path round the lake I see that I've either got to walk at least a mile along the back, or I could go the short way and cross the dam through the hard-hat men.

If I want to say hello.

The church bell bongs. I try to guess the time without looking at my phone, which is getting low on battery. We've been here two days – this is the third – and without something to do or someone to talk to, I will probably die.

Clambering to my feet I brush sweaty strands of grass from my elbows and knees. Opposite, the girl straightens up and picks up her binoculars. I pretend not to notice and stroll towards the dam. Two men in high-vis jackets have their backs to me. They're still stroking their chins and looking down at the village below. I step on to the dam, wandering past them and over to the other side of the water. I can see where all the sacks of rubble are propping the whole thing up.

"Hey. Boy!" a voice calls from behind me.

Turning, I see a woman who has followed me on to the dam. The sun is directly behind her, backlighting her triangle of thin hair, neither blonde nor grey. Perhaps it's what Mum calls tobacco tint. More exactly, nicotine yellow. Because she's more of a silhouette than a vision, I can't really see her face, but her voice sounds older. She points over to Mum.

"Have they found her then?" she shouts.

"Edith the Fair?" I shrug. "Dunno."

The woman nods her head. "Plenty of bodies."

"Just one, I think," I say.

"I don't mean there." Her voice lowers and she indicates the reservoir. "Here, and there." She waves her arm to include the woods and fields beyond. "I know for a fact there's one in that field."

"Really?" I ask, imagining burials behind every hedge. "Does anyone know?"

"Huh!" she says, turning back the way she came. "Not because I haven't told them. They only look things up on their gizmos. They don't listen to me."

"Oh?" I say.

"I've seen everything. All the goings-on."

"Really?"

"It goes back years. I've always said, always told 'em, but they don't pay a blind bit of notice. They think I'm away with the fairies, but I know what they say behind my back."

She's shaking her finger at me, and with every shake; the image of great archaeological discoveries fades. I've been taking her too seriously. "Sorry about that," I say.

I hear distant laughter. The woman swings round to look at my watcher.

"S'that girl," she says. "Always sneaking about in other people's business."

"What?" I say. But the woman's already scuttling off along the dam.

"I see you've met Newspaper Woman," says the girl when I finally wander over to where she's perched on a tree stump, barely in the shade. She has tight braids in her hair, lots of them, and she swings them round as she speaks so that they take off and land, pittering against each other.

"Newspaper Woman?"

"Yes. She lives by the church, catches the bus into town every day and brings back free newspapers. Dumps them at the pub because she thinks Granddad likes doing crosswords. So we call her Newspaper Woman." She waves a hand at me. "Hello, by the way. I'm Florence."

"I'm Daniel," I say. "Or Dan if you like."

"Hello, Dan. That's my sister, Emma," says Florence, pointing at the other girl. "Did Newspaper Woman tell you about the bodies in the fields?" She looks at me sideways. "D'you want to come swimming with us?"

"In that?" I point at the green ooze in front of us.

"No, in the river. It's lovely. Cold, though – do you mind cold? Emma'll come too. Won't you, Em?" She kicks her sister, who rolls over, still apparently glued to her screen. "She's not interested in what's going on here, only interested in stuff that comes through the airwaves." Florence points up at the sky as if a movie was going on about three metres over our heads. "She has a new boyfriend."

"Haven't," says Emma without looking up.

"Have — he's called Adam and he keeps lizards."

"Snakes."

Florence shivers. "Whatever. If he's interested in reptiles, he's a psychopath."

"What are you talking about?" asks Emma, sitting up and staring at her sister. She stares at me for the first time.

"Who's—" she begins.

"Dan, and he's coming swimming with us, aren't you, Dan?"

Chapter 2

"It was almost good. The dam so nearly burst," says
Florence, leading the way up a narrow path away
from the reservoir. There's a thin sort of shade, just
enough to produce flies that hover in small clouds,
but not really enough to cool the air. "But then
they panicked and evacuated everyone. They were
allowed back after the army dumped all the bags of
stuff on the dam, which was disappointing because
I thought something might actually happen here
for once."

"But if the dam had burst, wouldn't you have

lost everything?"

"We're from Bristol; we're only staying with Granddad now because Dad's away and Mum's working."

"So you weren't here?"

"No," says Florence, picking her way round a bramble. "Granddad sent us pictures. He took the photos off the wall. The rest of it would just be furniture and that."

"Still," I say. "Bit tragic."

"Yeah, s'pose. Now the water's almost gone and it's boring here. Sooooo boring. Although..." She beams at me. "You've arrived, so it's got a whole lot more interesting." She kicks off her sandals and I have a sudden panic that she's going to strip off her clothes and that this is going to involve nudity and that I am going to die of embarrassment.

Emma's stepping out of her sandals and dumping her phone next to them. I flinch as she undoes her shorts but she's wearing a swimming costume underneath. A second later she's sliding down over a tree branch until she's waist-deep in the river. "Ugh! So cold!" she shrieks as the water creeps up her body.

"Chicken!" shouts Florence. Pulling her dress over her head and kicking off her shoes, she leaps over Florence's head and bombs into the water right next to her sister. I slide down gently, letting the icy water slop up my calves, each hair on my legs releasing a bubble of air. I'm still not sure about getting my shorts wet, but the two girls are in, so I take my phone out of my pocket and throw it up on to the bank, letting myself slip into the water as far as my knees.

"Yay!" shouts Florence, slipping under the surface, startling a water bird from its hiding place along the river. "Lovely, isn't it?"

"Freezing," says Emma, lying on her back and kicking her legs out in the stream so that she stays steady in the flow. She's wearing a costume that glows through the water. The rest of her body is invisible against the river bed.

The river darkens a ring around the bottom of my shorts. This might be enough. I might not need to go any deeper, but Florence has other ideas and, making another huge leap, she cannons into me, sending me sprawling into the water.

* * *

Later, we lie in the sun, steaming.

"So is the body stuff really rubbish?" I ask.

"Yes," says Florence.

"No," says Emma.

"What?" asks Florence, sitting up and turning to her sister.

"I don't know for sure," says Emma, flipping the cover of her phone over. "But I'm pretty sure she used to have a husband."

"Newspaper Woman?"

"Yes – I don't remember him. It's always been just her. But she goes on about how one day he just disappeared."

"For real?" I ask.

"Well, she says he just walked out one day – and now she's always saying that there are bodies. So I'm guessing she killed him."

"Whoa," says Florence. "I didn't know that."

"I don't think he's the only one," says Emma. "She's probably killed loads of people. She's almost certainly a mass murderer. Anyway – I'm off." She stands and puts her shorts back on. The soggy costume seeps through, leaving a damp patch on her bum that makes it look like she's wet herself.

Florence and I follow. The crickets are noisier than ever, but I feel a whole lot better now I've been in the water, even if my shorts kind of chafe.

"Don't you know any more?" Florence calls after her sister.

"No," says Emma, and she breaks into a long-legged run, leaving us crunching through the dusty leaves until we reach the sheep-nibbled grass of the reservoir banks.

We stand blinking. The sun's lower but it's still majestically hot.

"This is the hottest summer for years. Or at least the longest drought since nineteen seventy-six, which was an epically dry year – actually over two years because they went sixteen months with no significant rainfall. This time it's only been eight weeks without rain – or it has here in Somerset. It'll be monsoon rains when the weather breaks – if it breaks." Florence peers into the reservoir.

The water's gone down a couple more centimetres, leaving a tide line and huge fissures in the muddy sides. I reach into my pocket in case there's a stray Lego figure. This mud is perfect. I could make a brilliant little movie with a figure in an enormous

Mars-scape. Although, glancing at Florence, maybe not in front of her. Maybe later.

In the distance Emma disappears into the shade on her way down to the village.

Florence starts writing her name in the mud with a stick.

"What's that?" I say, pointing towards the shore of the green water where there's a darker green square just breaking the surface.

Florence tilts her head to look. "Dunno," she says. "Perhaps it's a diving platform or something. Gotta go. See you tomorrow?"

"Suppose…"

"Great. Ten o'clock. By the way, don't eat anything from the freezer cabinet at the shop. Mr Hughes keeps dead birds for stuffing in there. You know, taxidermy. Bye."

"What?" But she runs away, leaving me staring at the square in the middle of the lake and feeling faintly like I've been hit around the head.

Mum's rented a cottage that's right below the dam at the top of the village. Everything about it is white, and it's got wooden signs on the wall that say things like "Life's a Beach" and "Keep Calm and Carry On". My room is at the back under a huge tree that drops sticky stuff on to the windows. I quite like the room, even though the cushions on the bed say "Happy Place" and "Work Hard and Dream Big" on them. I've turned them round, so now I'm just looking at buttons, which remind me of Coraline and are ever so slightly scary if my hands brush against them when it's dark.

When I come downstairs for breakfast, Mum's making coffee and the perfectly white kitchen worktop is growing brown rings. "Hopefully they'll come off with bleach," she says, peering at the set of Olympic circles and swiping at them with a cloth before running to answer the door.

"Cat," she says, throwing open the door and welcoming in a tall woman wearing wellies. Mum guides her towards the little terrace that overlooks the village, and rushes in to get the coffee.

"I've made a friend," she hisses. "Works on a farm – hoping she'll let us use the tractor to lift out the gravestone."

"Oh, OK," I say, selecting a bowl from the cupboard. Not sure whether I prefer "I Dream of

Unicorns" or "Go with the Flow". In the end I find one decorated with cutesy kittens and pour cereal into it.

Mum dashes through grabbing two mugs. "She wants to know if we can get DNA off those old bones. Why do people always want to know that? It's not like we know any of Edith the Fair's descendants."

I sit on the doorstep to eat my cereal so my feet are just in the sun.

"So what bit of the skeleton can you get DNA from?" asks Mum's friend.

"Teeth are good," says Mum. "But I doubt we'll get anything from our lady over there – she's too old and fragile. Been underwater for years, but I can find out about diet and things."

They talk about everyone doing DNA tests, and digging and bones and the past and family history, and why the graves are on the side of the reservoir, and gravestones, and generally the normal conversations that surround Mum. It's an occupational hazard talking about death.

Mum rushes past me to get the milk. "She says she can show me a path that leads from the burial site to the little church over at Amersdyke, which has a Saxon arch. Really very exciting. Going to move the first set of bones today. Do you want to come to the museum?" she asks, pouring the milk into a jug. "It's got air conditioning."

"I'm meeting this girl called Florence," I say, drinking the last drops of milk from my bowl. "We're going to look for bodies."

"Marvellous," says Mum, running outside with the milk. "Hope you find lots," she shouts over her shoulder from the front door.

It takes a couple of minutes to fill a water bottle and rummage in the cupboard for a half-eaten packet of biscuits. I stuff them in my backpack. I put my swimming trunks on under my shorts. Hot, but better than wet shorts or embarrassment. Standing at the kitchen sink, I can see the dam towering above us. It's massive from here. A sloping wall of stone with a house-sized jagged hole in it about halfway up. There are loads of those rubble bags that builders use, crammed with rocks and blocks, jammed in the hole. I'm guessing that this is what Florence was talking about, repairing the dam, but it strikes me that it's not really a repair so much as a sticking plaster. I can see where the cracks have run across the whole thing. This cottage would be right in the way if the dam collapsed. Still, they've taken quite a bit of the water out – it must be a whole lot lighter. I'm guessing they'll have fixed it by the time the autumn comes.

Upstairs, I check my phone. Dev and Jason are going to the cinema this afternoon to avoid the heat. Do I want to come? Yeah, sure – only five hours of train journeys between me and home. Next, I flick over a picture-postcard photo of golden sands and waving palm trees and realise that Kyle's grinning in the middle of it. He's in Jamaica. With his family, drinking things out of fresh coconuts. He's been snorkelling. The fish are amazing.

I turn off my screen. Probably better not to look.

"I'm off. Lock up when you go!" Mum shouts up the stairs.

A church bell bongs across the village – nine forty-five? I lock the front door and then, hoping that no one's watching me, jam the key under the flowerpot right by the door. This is safe as we're in the countryside. At least, that's what Mum says. She doesn't even lock the car here, which is just negligent in my opinion.

It's already sweltering and my T-shirt sticks my bag to my back the moment I start to clamber up the path towards the dam steps. I probably should have looked for a hat, or worn some suntan lotion, or made some attempt not to fry.

The chin-strokers are there again, more of them this time. And the green water is still pumping out into the soggy field at the side, although not so much and it's kind of thicker now. Small clusters of insects mass over the water and there are birds swooping through, chattering madly as if they know that soon it'll be too hot to even lift a wing. There are steps up to the dam on both sides, so I go to the nearest and climb slowly in the shade before emerging in the heat at the top. The view from up here is amazing. I can see over the houses in Sandford all the way down through little tufts of trees to the next village, which must be miles away. I'm level with the church spire here. If I could walk through the air, I'd be able to skim over the rooftops, even the village hall, which is covered in scaffolding.

Above me, on the hills, there are big birds circling, riding the air currents looking for small creatures below. I wander over to the centre of the dam and look down. A small amount of water is flowing down through a weir into the river below, but I can see that the level has dropped enough for them to start fixing the stonework in the reservoir. A collection of hot people in yellow jackets are lowering scaffolding into the water to build a tower. I watch. I'm kind of amazed to see how deep it still is. It would still be possible to hide a house under the water. Maybe even a whole collection of houses. Someone drops the end of a piece of rope that goes down and down and down. Twenty metres or so.

I look up to see if Florence's arrived. She's not on her tree roots yet. On the other side of the water Mum, Anya and David are fussing around a stretcher that must be for the bones.

I could go and see, but they're just bones and although sometimes the stories that go with the bones are really interesting, it always takes ages, and I've usually forgotten who the person was that Mum was looking for when she finds out the results. They're mysteries, but really slow mysteries.

I'm hoping that Newspaper Woman and her bodies might be more productive. But I don't even know exactly where Newspaper Woman lives. Or her name or anything. I suppose I could go and look around the village.

Ten bongs.

And the quarter bong.

Perhaps I *should* go towards the village? Perhaps Florence's forgotten. Perhaps she's really flaky.

I'm dithering when she comes running towards me over the dam, her sandals slapping the stone and her hair bouncing. Alongside her bounds a small dog that barrels into my legs and starts sniffing my feet and then looks up at me expectantly.

"Sorry, sorry – late because of the washing-up, which was Emma's fault."

"S'fine. Hello, dog," I say, putting my hand out.

The dog ignores the hand; it's definitely more interested in feet. I don't really understand dogs.

"Emma's gone on the bus to town with Adam. Tony, our uncle, says it's a holiday romance – it won't last. How was your night? How were the sausages you had for tea? Oh, and this is Squish. He's Granddad's dog. I'm training him to be a truffle hound."

"How d'you know we had sausages?"

"Oh, I know everything. Anyway, I asked Granddad about Newspaper Woman and the bodies." She begins to walk off the bridge and I follow, still trying to work out how she knew what we ate last night.

"Granddad was vague but he said it's true that she goes on about having had a husband – and that she says he disappeared, and she's got this thing about telling people that there are dead bodies everywhere." Florence gazes into the distance as if she might see a body rearing from the ground. "But no one believes her. She's a total pain because of the newspapers, and every winter she tells everyone to open their cupboards so that their pipes won't freeze. What else did he say? Oh yeah, her name is Laura Barlow."

While she's talking, I'm staring at the lake. The water's gone down some more, and now the platform near the shore that looked completely flat yesterday is more obvious, and it's slightly curved.

"Looks like a car roof," I say.

"Yeah," she says. "Shall we go and look in the woods and see if we can find any of her victims? And maybe we could jump in the river at the same time."

Chapter 3

It's the middle of the night and unbearably hot, but if I open the window, the mosquitoes that must be breeding in the lake above flood into my room. I've bounced around on the bed swatting them. I reckon I've got them all, and now I've got the window closed.

I do probably sleep, but the night seems to take forever so I overthink everything that happened yesterday. Well, not much did happen yesterday. It was hot, and Florence and I crashed around in the bushes looking for bodies, and mushrooms and early blackberries, and in an attempt to cool down we ended up in the river with Squish. She made him sniff some old tree fungus, which made him sneeze, and then he ate it. We talked about our lives, about where we live, about Sandford being so different from the city. She talked about her parents and Emma; and I talked about Mum, about living with Mum, about how close we are. She asked about my dad and I told her I didn't have one, didn't know who he was and didn't really care. That Mum never mentioned him and I didn't ask because Mum was enough parent for one child. I asked what it was like having a sister. She said it wasn't all it was cracked up to be; she could cheerfully send Emma off in a boat to the other side of the world but that she probably loved her really.

It was fun, it was actually really fun, having someone my own age to hang out with and do just about whatever we wanted, and it was fun wandering around the countryside, even if it was a million degrees hot. But now I can feel the first bites starting to itch and I'm thinking about all that water lying in those fields on the other side of the reservoir and I'm imagining giant mosquitoes breeding there. I think we're living in a hot swamp. Sort of like the Amazon – but with no alligators.

When morning arrives it's already hot before the church bell even bongs seven. There's a bite on my ankle the size of a small egg and I limp downstairs to the kitchen and slap a lump of ice on it.

Mum appears a moment later. "Couldn't sleep?" I nod.

"Me neither," she says, flipping the switch on the kettle. "Is your friend around today?"

"She's off buying shoes or something," I answer, waiting for the bite to stop itching.

"Stuck with me then," says Mum. "We're just investigating the area to the right of the grave. Anya thinks there might be another burial, but it gets horribly hot out there in the open. We may have to wait for the weather to break."

We eat toast listening to the radio. The weather forecast is hot, with added hot. They reckon Scotland will be hotter than Ireland, and England will be hotter than both.

My feet covered in tea tree oil and all the skin in between coated with insect repellent, we set off up to the dam, trickles of sweat already setting off down the back of my neck.

I spend the whole day sitting and watching Mum and the team scraping a centimetre of earth from a pit. They sweat. In the absolute hottest part of the day we lie in the shade and eat pots of salad from Mr Hughes' shop. With each mouthful I think about the dead birds he keeps in the freezer and the salad becomes less delicious. I look out at the reservoir, watching the water slowly drain. The thing at the side is definitely a car roof.

During the afternoon the woman I now know is called Laura Barlow comes to the dam and stares into the water. She talks to the chin-strokers and then visits the dig. At first I don't think she's actually coming over, she takes such tiny steps and moves so lightly over the burned grass, but she stops about twenty metres away and peers at us. "You want to go and dig up those fields if you're after bodies," she says.

"We've got one here – do you want to come and see?" asks Dave, straightening up and moving over to greet her. "You're very welcome."

"Ooh my, no," says Mrs Barlow, flapping the idea

away. "Bones. I don't like bones. My bodies are newer bodies. Recent. Only a few years ago." She leans in closer. "Thick as thieves they were," she whispers.

She points at the field and the woods and the reservoir. He nods as if he's really interested but when she turns away he returns to the dig, shaking his head. She stares after him, watching him crouch back down by the dig. Eventually she retreats to the dam, gives the water one last look and shuffles back towards the village.

At sunset, Florence and Squish come to join me with two packets of crisps and two bottles of ice-cold homemade elderflower fizz.

"That was horrible. Town was so hot and Emma is a witch." Florence ties knots in a strand of grass. "I could kill her sometimes. Still, we're here now. Cheers!" We clank our bottles together and Mum and the team crack open bottles of beer and eat crisps while scraping at the earth. It's a party and a dig both at once. As the sun drops, a couple of people from the village join in as volunteer diggers. Mum's new friend Cat, Florence's uncle Tony, and a bloke with very long hair who might be called Shane or Shame, I can't work it out. Apparently he once worked on an archaeological dig in Egypt. Whatever, he needs to wash his armpits or change his T-shirt or both. Tony has brought a guitar and plays it well and he knows loads of songs. The tunes circle over the lake and bounce back from the trees. It's kind of magical, even in the heat, and I lean back on the grass and try not to scratch my bites.

"When I was a nipper we used to sit out here and tell stories," says Uncle Tony. "Dad had lots, mostly about sleeping knights under Old Westerthwaithe." He gestures towards the distant hills.

"Most places have that story," says Mum. "My grandmother used to talk about knights sleeping in the Welsh borders. They were going to come and save us from disaster."

"*Bedknobs and Broomsticks*," says Cat. "Isn't that about knights saving everyone from disaster?"

They laugh and I try to remember the film. I must have seen it, surely?

Cat's talking again. "My mum brought us here for holidays and always told us stories of buried treasure."

Above us a cloud of birds cluster and break and flow over the trees. Amazing.

"Probably the knights guarding the treasure," says Shane/Shame.

"S'nice here," says Florence. "Although, be better with a really good thunderstorm. The last time it did that was in May and in Bristol our street filled with water. But I love a snow day, really. Don't you? Dan, you know that thing you've been looking at? It's really sticking up now. It's definitely a car."

In spite of the last rays of the sun blinding us over the reservoir, I can see that not only is it a car, but we can actually see inside. Kind of. The water level appears to be below the ceiling.

"Let's go and get a better look," I say to Florence, and we stumble over the muddy shoreline and scrabble our way up on to the dam. It's dusk, it's hard to see, the reflections from the water are weird, and there are clouds of midges brushing around our heads.

"One of the windows is open, isn't it?" says Florence, leaning out from the parapet of the dam.

We strain to make out what we're looking at.

"Is that. . .?" she asks.

"I don't know," I say, staring so hard through the gloom that my eyeballs hurt. "It might be." I fumble with my phone, but the torch isn't strong enough to make a difference. "There's something inside."

"Or someone," says Florence.

"Mum!" I shout across the reservoir. "Mum!"

But she's not listening.

"Mum!" My voice bounces around between the trees and birds take off, wheel and land again, but Mum and the others are happy chatting in the cool of the evening and it's us who can hear them, not the other way around.

"I'll get her," says Florence, already running back along the dam and down the steps.

While she's gone I lean as far as I can and try again to see through the fading light – it's darker inside the car, like there is something that isn't just eels or weed, but it's tantalisingly too far away to be sure. I take a pic with my phone and try zooming in on it, but it's grainy and indistinct.

As I try to make sense of the shapes I can see, the final strand of sunset blinks out at the top of the trees and the darkness becomes thick so that only white things show. Florence's white T-shirt. Mum's white hat. The white tent over the dig.

"What?" says Mum to Florence, their voices bouncing through the darkness. "A body? Are you sure?"

Thing is, we're not sure.

Uncertain, we glance at each other as we tell the policeman who comes to the cottage. He's meeting us here because it was going to take hours. They told Mum that when she rang. And they were right. I've almost forgotten what I saw when he finally turns up. There's just one policeman because apparently there's a wedding fight going on at a hotel in town and the remaining two police officers are caught up in that. He probably thought he had the easy job coming to see us, but he hasn't met Florence.

He takes off his hat and scratches his head. He's had his hair cut recently and they've trimmed his sideburns so that one's shorter than the other. I wonder if he knows. Also, there's a thin trail of sweat that's still moving down his face, just in front of his ear. "You sure there was something inside?" he says.

"Definitely," says Florence.

"And the first time you saw anything at all suspicious was this evening?"

"Just as the light went," I say. "We ran up to the dam, but my phone torch isn't strong enough to see very far. We saw a dark patch inside the car."

The policeman nods as he writes. His pencil scratch, scratches on the page.

"I mean, it can't actually be a body, can it?" Mum watches us from the doorway, looking distracted and vaguely anxious.

The policeman shrugs. "I'll go up with my torch in a bit – see what I can see."

"Couldn't you go now?" says Florence.

"I'm asking you questions just now," he says.

Florence pinches her mouth together and sits on her hands as if they're the things that keep on making her interrupt.

"But isn't it urgent?" I say.

"It's not going anywhere," says Mum.

The policeman doesn't reply.

"Yes, but if there's someone in there—" Florence begins.

"And is there anything else apart from a car?" The policeman looks up at me. "Anything?"

Florence shrugs. I can't think of anything else to say.

The policeman stands up and goes to the door. "Thank you then," he says.

"Is that it?" asks Florence. "Aren't you going to call in a SWAT team or something?"

For the first time the policeman smiles. "I am not. I *will* walk up with my torch. I *am* going to make a couple of phone calls and then I'll call in at the hotel and hopefully go home for my tea."

Florence's face falls into a deep frown. "But that's—"

"Life," finishes the policeman, putting his cap back on his head and pulling open the front door. "Goodnight, all," he says, and he steps out into the dark.

Chapter 4

It's another hot night. This time there's definitely a mosquito in my room. Probably the same one that left the enormous bite on my foot. It's full of my blood and I'm not letting it have any more. I pull the duvet over my head and slowly suffocate.

I cannot stop thinking about the car.

And whatever was inside it.

Or wasn't.

But we both saw something. Didn't we?

At about five I give up the sleep business and reach for my phone to message Florence.

You awake?

No reply, so, as the light begins to grow, I get up. The sun's not actually beating down yet, but it will soon. For now the morning belongs to snuffling things and spiders and noisy birds.

I pull on shorts and a T-shirt and tiptoe downstairs. I leave a note for Mum. *Gone for a walk.* And I slide out of the front door into the cool morning. There's dew and tiny cobwebs on every bush and tussock. The air is damp and smells of earth and grass and summer. It's so refreshing after the relentless heat that I wonder why I don't get up at this time every morning – and then I remember that normally I sleep.

The steps up to the reservoir are damp. Everything's damp, but the moment the sun gallops over the horizon, the moisture vanishes, the dark earth turns dusty and the heat rises. The first actual sunbeams hit my bare arms and I can feel just how hot it is already.

I stop halfway up the steps and look back at the village. The mist hangs in thick curtains across the valley. You could imagine that the church spire and the pub roof were sticking out of the sea, that all around was an enormous flood. I take the last couple of steps and I'm up on the dam. It's a concrete bridge through the clouds on either side. Dense whiteness below and thin strands of grey above. Three geese stand on the mud honking and flapping their wings. Beyond them, the car.

I stop in the middle of the dam and stare hard. The car isn't really a colour. Perhaps it's silver, perhaps blue. And the window on the driver's side is rolled down about a quarter. It's covered in tufts of green. Small wisps of weed, clinging to the glass, but there's light coming through the windscreen and I can now quite clearly see the headrest.

With nothing leaning against it.

Nothing?

Oh, man – I was so sure there was something there. I look back at my phone and try to compare the murky picture I took last night with what I can see now.

Yeah, definitely something darker in front of the headrest. But it could be weed. A load of weed that's sunk with the water as the level's gone down. Or it could be a big fish that's not moving. Or perhaps it's eels. A massive knot of eels.

Or it could be a head.

I'm leaning against the rail, staring at the car, when I hear the sound of an engine and an SUV pulls to a halt at the top of the road from the village. It's black, like super-shiny black.

Two people get out and blink in the sunshine. One's a middle-aged woman in a fleece and jeans. She's holding a coffee mug. The other's a younger man in jeans who goes round to the back of the car and puts on a pair of wellington boots.

Even without uniforms they're obviously police officers. They're too neat to be anything else.

I wave, and at first they ignore me.

"There," I point. "There."

The woman nods and gestures at the car's roof, now showing quite clearly over the water. The man still doesn't seem to have spotted it. Instead he's poking his toe at the mud round the sides of the reservoir. The woman joins him. They really don't seem that interested.

"Come on!" I say, jumping up and down and waving at them until they finally start to walk across the top of the dam. "This way – hurry."

"Oh – it's a car," says the woman, stopping beside

me to look into the water.

Der, I think. But don't say it.

"It's quite deep in there. We might need some help," she says, reaching into her pocket for a mobile phone and then putting it back in her pocket.

"Are you the kid that called it in?" says the man, stepping up on to the dam and leaning over the rail to stare at the car.

"One of them," I say.

"OK, I'm DC Boyle and this is DS Patel."

DS Patel passes me, wanders down the far side and tries tiptoeing over the mud but it's soft and after a couple of steps she's kind of wading. It oozes over her shoes.

"Looks like it's been there a while," says DC Boyle, following her down but staying well clear of the mud. He unrolls a car length of police tape and looks in his pocket for something to act as a tent peg. Finding a pencil, he snaps it in two and uses it to skewer the tape to the ground.

"What'll happen next?" I ask.

"We'll get a tractor in to pull it out and you'll keep well away," he says, muttering something into his radio and helping his colleague out of the mud.

Sitting on the top of the dam, I wait for a tractor to arrive. After two hours, I'm wavering between staying and going, when Florence arrives.

"How long you been here then? Ages?" she asks, and then goes on without waiting for an answer. "I've had breakfast, scrambled eggs and avocado. It was mint, if you're asking— I reckon that Mrs Barlow recognises that car."

"What?"

"Look," she says, pointing over to the steps at the end of the dam.

She's right. Mrs Barlow has arrived and is holding her hand over her mouth and looks even paler than usual. She grips the rail and says something I can't hear, first quietly to herself and then louder, leaning over towards DC Boyle.

He shakes his head as if he wants her to go away, but she looks determined. Eventually she takes something out of her bag and waves it at him.

"What is that?" asks Florence.

"It's a bit of paper," I say. "A photo?"

A distant engine has been getting steadily louder and the policeman raises his head to listen.

He ignores Mrs Barlow and the flapping photo. Instead he goes to greet the tractor driver. It's a big blue tractor and the driver stops it just at the water's edge without killing the engine. Mrs Barlow shouts at the policeman's back and goes on waving her piece of paper at him.

"What's she saying?" I ask Florence.

"Dunno," she says. "It's Tim? It's him, maybe?"

DC Boyle seems determined not to listen to her.

"It's his car," she shouts. Each word distinct. We hear her, but there's no way the policeman's going to catch her words as he's standing right next to the tractor. His colleague is nowhere to be seen.

"Look, she's gone quiet," says Florence as DC Boyle takes a heavy-looking chain from the tractor driver and wades carefully into the water.

By the time he reaches the back of the car, it must be well over the top of his wellingtons but he fumbles around under the water and then stands and waves, stepping back.

Mrs Barlow is silent. She's watching the car, its roof trembling as the chain tightens.

The tractor revs and the chain strains, and then slowly, really slowly, the car kind of skis out of the reservoir, while waterfalls of green water pour out under the doors. It scrapes over the mud, wheels locked, gouging two lines behind it. A wash of thick gloop sloshes back into the reservoir.

"Stop!" shouts DC Boyle, holding his hand high.

"Oh my word!" says Mrs Barlow, her hands back by her mouth. It's not much more than a whisper, but I hear it, and I can see that she's seeing a whole lot more than a filthy old car.

The car sinks a little, but it doesn't seem to want to run back into the water. Now that it's out we can see what kind of car it is. It's a car-shaped car. Four doors, all the windows. It's a light greeny-sandy colour, all of which has probably been added by living submerged in a lake. It's even still got tyres. Although they're flat.

His boots leaking water from the top, DC Boyle steps up to the passenger door and tries to open it, but the handle appears to have fused. He gives it a good yank, then gives up and with his head sideways, peers in through the top of the window.

I watch him tilt his head from side to side, examining the interior.

He shouts something back at DS Patel, who has

miraculously reappeared now that the car's out of the mud.

"What?" she yells.

"Nothing," he shouts. "There's nothing there! S'empty!"

They put the blue tape all round the car and chat to the tractor driver. More people come and stare, and Mrs Barlow clambers down from the dam and walks round the side of the reservoir.

I can't hear the conversation, but I can see that she's upset. She points at the car, and back at the village, and she waves her photo, and she begins to cry and DS Patel takes her off to sit on the dry grass at the top.

Before long Cat joins them, putting her arm round Mrs Barlow's shoulder and offering her tissues. DS Patel leaves them together and goes to peer at the car.

Florence does a long inward sigh. "Nothing in there?" she says. "But..."

"So did I," I say. "I definitely saw something."

"Which means that we were having a collective hallucination or it dissolved?"

"Or swam away?"

"Er, yuk, like eels or something? Or it was floating and has gone down with the water level and is lying on the seat."

"Weed?"

She nods.

"Or it means that someone moved it so that it wouldn't be found."

Florence stares at me. "How?"

"I don't know, but I'm going to think about it."

Chapter 5

Mum is not that happy that I went off this morning.

But she's not that happy anyway because she's got a hangover and it's already nearly thirty degrees. "Don't just go off without telling me," she says banging old coffee grounds into the bin. "I was worried."

"Were you?" I ask.

She stops, and smiles. "I wasn't, actually, but I felt I ought to be. After all, we don't know the people in this village, or our way around."

"You know Cat and I know Florence. And we've

sort of met Mr Hughes from the shop and there's Florence's granddad in the pub, and the Shane person."

"Don't mention him; it was his dodgy cider that did this to my head."

"And Florence's uncle, Tony."

"Is he the man with the guitar? Anyway, that's beside the point. You must tell me where you are."

"You could have texted," I say, "if you were that worried."

Mum laughs and drops the coffee pot. "Oh, I am hopeless," she says. "Make me some coffee, Dan. Make it strong."

We wander up to the dig. There are two more archaeologists and a few volunteers. Shane is back. He's wearing a clean T-shirt, definitely less stinky. Also Cat, who says she's able to help for the morning, and seems really interested in the dig, but honestly anyone out here after twelve must be a masochist. Add to that two silent sisters, who are uni students, and me.

Yes, me.

I want an excuse to be near the car, and the dig is the perfect excuse. Also, because now Mum is worried that when the weather breaks the site will be lost forever she's keen to check out as many test pits as possible before that happens and actually wants my help.

From here I can see Mrs Barlow still sitting up at the top of the bank. She's well away from the other people and still seems to be crying. Every now and then DS Patel comes to sit with her but soon gets bored and wanders off. The policewoman doesn't seem to be taking any notes. Perhaps she thinks everything that Mrs Barlow says is stories. Perhaps she already knows her.

But I'm not so sure.

"Right, everyone – let's work in teams of three. We're going to start on the two pits marked out to the east. We're looking for buildings, walls, anything that might show that this was a monastery or a church."

I crouch at the top corner, trowel in hand, and look over to the car. I can now see the other side of it, the driver's side, and it's far less evenly covered in weed than the dam side. Squinting at it, it seems there are bright-blue scratches around the door handle, as if the years of algae have been rubbed off and the real paint is showing underneath, and when a police person in an all-over white suit thing tries to pull on the handle, the door actually opens.

I wonder if I missed someone making those scratches. There was an hour between me going home and coming back on the dig.

For a long time I can't see anything very much except white-clad bums leaning over the car seats. Then they load some stuff into trays, but I can't see what it is. Between times, I scrape the soil, slowly sinking layer by layer through the dried mud. There's a lot of mud and it's baked hard. I spend fifteen minutes shuffling dust into a dustpan and pouring it through a sieve, and when I finish that Mrs Barlow seems to have gone. So does the policewoman.

"If we can all work on this trench, which is nearer the water, then it might buy us a day or so if the weather breaks..." Mum's talking.

Over on the dam, lots of people are now watching the motionless car, including Florence. She's holding a pair of binoculars. Shame she's the wrong side, though. I wonder if she can see anything useful?

There are also loads of journalists taking photos with huge cameras. I bet they can see everything.

"Dan?" says Mum, bellowing in my ear. "Are you concentrating? Did you hear anything I said?"

It's too hot after twelve thirty, even in the shade of the trees, so we set off in a long line to the pub, where there's an ancient dank courtyard garden that suddenly seems attractive. Everyone's red; some of us burned by the sun, the rest of us just hot. I'm gritty too, earth between my fingers and toes, and I keep on imagining the river. Jumping in. Splashing. Water over my shoulders, my head. Just washing my feet and hands would be pretty amazing. As we trail off, I glance back at the car, which is dry on the outside. The police and scene-of-crime people are all sagging in the shade at the top of the bank. But none of them look very excited. Perhaps there was nothing to find.

Florence's disappeared too. I wonder if she discovered anything.

The garden at the back of the pub is hot, but so much cooler than the reservoir. Large trees hang over the yard and apart from a lazy wasp and a faint smell of old fish, it's the closest thing to heaven around here. The diggers all settle around two tables and start to unwrap sandwiches and drink huge long glasses of shandy. Mum goes to the bar and orders us a scampi and chips to share, along with icy glasses of lime juice and soda. I down half of mine until I feel that cold headachy thing on the back of my neck and have to run inside and stick my head under the cold tap so that I don't faint.

"Heatstroke," yells Dave from the table.

I stand in the loos and splash my face until I stop feeling sick.

The door opens behind me. "You OK?"

It's Florence and Squish, standing in the doorway.

"This is the gents," I say.

"S'OK," she says. "No one cares. Guess what I heard? Actually, not here," she says, grabbing my elbow. "Follow me."

"I thought it didn't matter," I say.

"Let's try the kitchen," she says, leading the way down a dark corridor into a room lined with freezers and microwaves.

"This is a kitchen?"

"Everything goes from freezer to microwave

here. Granddad's never heard of cooking. Mum's appalled because it says home-cooked on the menu. So's Uncle Tony – he thinks it's going to land Granddad in trouble, but he still sticks lots of stuff in the microwave." She stares at a pie going round and round. "Disgusting. Anyway – the car – they're all talking about it. Lots of suggestions about how it got there. Did you find anything out?"

I get out my phone and flick through the pictures. I hold it up to Florence and point at the blue scratches surrounding the door handle of the car. "See – this is on the other side. The side away from the dam."

"Oh!" she says, enlarging the picture. "Do you think those are recent?"

"They have to be, don't they? Everything else is covered in green slime. This bit's been cleaned off. But they could have been made by the police. They might have forced the driver's door while I was home at the cottage having breakfast."

"I don't know," says Florence, staring out into the garden. "I was there after you left. They just stuck a tape round it. They didn't try the other door, I don't think. Although – I dunno – I wish

I could remember."

"Did you see anything with the binoculars? I saw you looking."

"No, but they took lots of samples from the mud at the bottom of the car. They didn't seem to find anything much though. I expect it takes weeks to go through it all. You know, sorting the amoeba from the bits of car. Oh!" She bobs excitedly as she remembers more. "It's a Ford car, and I got the number plate. It was..." She checks her phone.

The pie pings in the microwave.

"XDF 396 T or J?"

"Florence! Get out of the way!" A woman with scraped-back hair and no eyebrows brushes past us. "And no non-staff in here. You know the rules."

"Non-staff?" Florence rolls her eyes and does an exaggerated jaw drop. "It's just my friend Dan. Dan, meet Aimee. She basically runs the pub for Granddad."

"You can't get round me like that. Get out of here." Aimee drives us out of the microwave space with the flick of a tea towel and we shuffle back down the corridor. Florence sits on the bottom of some carpeted stairs, patting the space beside her.

"Ooh, you're still in the way." Aimee steps over our ankles with two plates of pie and peas for someone in the bar.

"So when did Laura Barlow's husband disappear?" I ask. "And who was he?"

Florence shrugs. "Granddad will know — let's ask."

We don't really need to ask. All the locals are in the bar, talking, while the tourists and the diggers are outside. It's weird standing here among the mismatched chairs and the black-and-white photos of long-dead cricket teams. They're not actually staring at me, but it feels as if they are.

"Poor Laura if it is his car," says a woman sitting up at the bar. "I mean, what a shock! All those years wondering if he's driven off with his fancy woman."

"She's been on about him being in the ground forever — least I think it was him," says a man. "Unless there's lots of bodies around here we don't know about!" He laughs, but no one joins in.

The soft hiss of pints being drawn fills the silence.

"Can't remember his name just now."

"Ian? Was it? Or Simon?"

They shake their heads.

"I do feel for her. Poor thing. So lonely living all on her own all these years."

"Like lots of other people in this village, no friends, no family."

There's more silence and I step backwards towards the door. It's awkward in the middle of this circle of locals chatting.

"Yeah, but it's only a car," says Florence's Uncle Tony. "Not a body – they've not found a thing in there."

"Clothing's what I heard."

"Clothing?"

Everyone rumbles their surprise.

Florence slips behind the bar and leans over the top.

"What?" says her granddad, looking down at her.

"When did her husband disappear?" she asks.

"Ah," he says. "When did he go then? Laura's husband – anyone remember?"

"The long hot summer," says someone. "Definitely – so what year was that?"

"The drought? Nineteen seventy-six," says Cat, coming in with two glasses. "I was five that summer. It was so hot, and so dry – Mum said it might never rain again. I remember doing a rain dance in the garden with a friend."

"Could the car be nineteen seventy-six – you sure?" Florence asks the room. "The number plate was XDF 396 J or T?"

"That's a seventies plate, definitely," says Uncle Tony. "I was a kid then too. I used to collect number plates."

"So what happened here in nineteen seventy-six?" I ask the room. This time they do all stare at me.

There's a long silence. A dog under a table scratches and licks some spilled beer.

"Curiosity killed the cat," says Florence's granddad, blocking the doorway back into the bar. "Don't know why you're asking so many questions, but it's not your business, young lady – or yours." He waves us away, and we head back along the dark corridor to the door marked Beer Garden.

"Sorry," says Florence. "That's Granddad telling me off. He doesn't normally mind me being nosy. Perhaps I should get Emma to ask questions but she's off drooling over Adam somewhere with air conditioning." We stop just inside the pub.

"I bet someone in there knows more," I say.

"Perhaps Mrs Barlow's husband ran away and put his car in the lake hoping she'd think he'd drowned when he'd actually just abandoned her," says Florence. "I mean, she is so annoying."

"Yeah," I say without thinking, but drifting outside, and stopping by the open window from the bar.

"What's the—"

"Shhh," I say, holding up my hand, because now we're gone the conversation's picked up back inside the bar.

"Thinking back to nineteen seventy-six," says the old man's voice. "Someone did disappear that year. But I can't remember who or where from. It might have been her husband."

There's a long silence, I nearly give up and then someone says, "Don't know how Laura Barlow ended up living there by the church. House used to belong to old Kenneth Fear. Remember?"

"That's it," says Florence's granddad. "It was nineteen seventy-six — she's right, that's the year they buried old Kenneth Fear. Ground was iron hard. They took him out of the back of that house."

"I remember that! Mechanical digger in the churchyard and the grave digger nearly resigned. He caught his head on the bucket, blood everywhere."

"Oh – of course." There's some more silence. Then someone says. "Shocking."

"Reservoir went green that year too."

"Not as empty as now, though."

"Yes, but, to be fair, the dam wasn't about to collapse."

"Ken died there on his own, didn't he? Sad," says a female voice. "I wonder if there was ever a Mrs Fear."

"Yup – there was," says Florence's granddad. "And there were kids. Recall some bother with one of the lads. Thomas. Got caught up with a bunch of villains. They put him away for a while. The daughter got out – she married someone from outside the village."

"I remember Ken, difficult old man," says one of the men. "Argued with everyone about everything."

"Liked the cider."

"Don't we all."

Everyone laughs and I sink down so that I'm leaning against the bottom of the wall but I can still hear.

"Wasn't that the year of the bullion robbery at Heathrow Airport?"

"That was it. That was what the lad was part of, wasn't it? Thomas Fear. He got twenty years, didn't he?"

"Something like. Moved up country afterwards."

"Oh yes, and there was a plague of ladybirds. All over the shop they were."

They all laugh again, and then they move back to talking about raising money for the village hall, but I'm turning the words over and over in my head.

Recall some bother with one of the lads. Thomas. Got caught up with a bunch of villains. They put him away for a while...
That was what the lad was part of, wasn't it? Thomas Fear.

I'm already googling Heathrow Airport bullion robbery and Thomas Fear when Florence straightens up alongside me. "I've had a thought," she says. "Meet me in ten in the car park." She smiles and disappears back into the depths of the pub and I hear her feet on the stairs.

Chapter 6

Back with the diggers I bolt my half of the scampi and while Mum's not paying proper attention, mumble something about going swimming and join Florence in the pub car park. My Google search gave me nothing useful, but I'll have another go later on. Beneath our feet the tarmac is scorching. I can feel it through my trainers, and everything smells hot, like it could burst into flames at any moment.

"This way," Florence says, slipping round the side of the pub and crossing the road. Ahead of me she dives along an overgrown path that runs along the back of a small playground. I slow down, stepping gingerly over an arching bramble, and when I look up Florence is disappearing round a long, low wall. I trot after her; the sun is ferocious and I'm dripping sweat by the time I catch up with her. I think, if we'd just walked along the lane we'd have reached the same place, but perhaps she doesn't want her granddad to see where we're going.

"Shh," she says, crouching. "There."

In front of us is the churchyard. Like most churchyards it's crammed with ancient graves at amazing angles deep in the shade of giant yew trees. "What am I looking at?"

"That house, over there. It's where Laura Barlow lives."

There's a house with its wall built into the graveyard wall. It has a bleached blue door on the churchyard side that looks as if no one has opened it for years, while the front of the house faces out into the lane. Everything about it is rundown, even the garden, where a couple of white butterflies are dancing around each other and a tall yellow weedy flower.

"No wonder she's got a thing about dead bodies – living in the middle of this lot," I say. "Walk past the front?"

We try to look nonchalant. Which is tricky in the boiling heat when no one else is around and they're all hiding indoors with giant glasses of iced water. A very dry leaf blows slowly in front of us up the lane, tossed on a breeze that I totally can't feel. When we're level with the front of Laura's house, I lean down and pick an imaginary stone from my trainers. Looking to the side, I see Laura emerge from the front of her house with a pair of scissors. She cuts something from a bush savagely. Angrily. She looks sad, but then she always looks sad. She glances across and catches sight of Florence.

"You saw," she says, her voice quiet, hissing as if she doesn't want to be overheard.

"Hello," says Florence.

"You saw the car."

"Er, yes," says Florence, glancing around. "I did."

"Did you see him?" Laura's garden gate creaks and she steps out of her garden and across the lane towards us, waving her scissors. Her eyes are

62

wide and her hair wilder than the last time I saw her. She's wearing an apron over a dressing gown, and I realise that her veined white feet are bare. She glances back at her house. "Did you see him inside?"

"We don't know what we saw." Florence falters and takes a pace back, giving me a hard stare like I'm going to rescue her. "Really not sure."

"You did or you didn't?" Mrs Barlow looks from me to Florence and back to me. "It's important. Was he there?"

"I don't know," I say, trying to be honest. "I thought I saw someone, but the seat was empty when they pulled the car out."

"They think I'm a fool," she says, staring at the cracks in the paving. And then, as if she's suddenly remembered something, she puts the scissors in her pocket and moves close to Florence, reaching out to touch her elbow. "You two, you need to be careful." She glances back to her house, gives Florence an almost smile, and scuttles back into the house before closing the door.

Florence lets out a long breath. "Whoa," she says. "That was intense."

"She's really upset."

Florence rolls her eyes. "Yeah, but she was scary too. And she had scissors."

"Something weird's going on. Did you see the way she kept on looking back at her house, like there was someone in there?" Pretending to find some interesting lichen on the wall, I look up towards Mrs Barlow's house. An upstairs curtain flickers.

For a moment we stay out in the open in front of her house, and I get the strongest feeling that people are watching us. I look up at the windows of the cottages on either side, but there's no one around. I look over to the scaffolding on the village hall. There's no one there. Even so, I feel exposed here in the middle of the road and I convince myself that I'm really curious to see where the famous Kenneth Fear was buried.

"C'mon," I say, turning back towards the churchyard. "Let's get out of here."

It's only a couple of steps to the churchyard gate and we walk in silence. Until Florence says, "What she said — that means it's definitely her husband's car, and she thinks he's inside."

I think about it as we push the gate open. "Or he WAS inside. She expected him to be inside."

The grass of the churchyard is burned yellow and crunches under our feet. Tiny blue butterflies dance in the wild margin of the enclosure, but otherwise it feels paused as if it's waiting for something.

I shudder. I don't normally mind graveyards, but there's something about this one, even in the middle of the day, that I don't like. Dark patches cluster under the trees around the sides, and some of the graves are split, thrown open by earth movement. Under the stones lurk black caverns. Also, it's really big; it goes off to the side and I can't see the end. Florence's reading out names. I walk along another row, reading them in my head. Spray, Curtis, Laverstock, D'eath. I stop and try to make sense of the name, read that one lots of times. Weird.

We wander out of the ancient graves towards the newer ones. The majority have ugly granite stones, and they're much more depressing than the pretty old ones. A couple have flowers, but they're largely neglected. Most of the occupants died in the nineteen sixties and seventies. Morland, Savage,

Rossetti, next one is Hancock, then Fear.

"Here," I say. "It's here."

"What?" says Florence, wandering over, and I point, reading the inscription aloud. "*Kenneth Fear, 1900 to 1976.*"

His stone is straight and his grave flat where most of the others in the row are sunken as if the ground underneath them has collapsed, but Kenneth Fear's grave was built on firmer foundations.

"Look," I say. "Kenneth Fear – the man who died the same year as Laura Barlow's husband disappeared? The man in the lake."

"Yeah," she says. "Kenneth, the man who was buried in the hot summer. And...?"

"I dunno, but somehow I think they're connected – and look." I point at the battered door at the back of Mrs Barlow's house. "The door's just there."

"That really means nothing." Florence crouches forward and brushes some long dead flowers to one side.

"*The lord giveth and the lord taketh away,*" she says, reading the stone. "Ah, but then there's something else written here. It's been kind of rubbed off."

The stone is extra bobbly, extra rough, like

someone tried to chip the letters off by hand when they didn't really know what they were doing.

"What does it say?" She rubs harder but it's really unclear.

"Brother?" I say. "It definitely says 'ther'."

"Hmm," says Florence, loping over to the tap by the compost heap. "Gonna try putting some water on it."

I join her and we fill our hands with tepid water and run back to the stone, throwing the water on to the granite, and briefly the letters show more clearly. "*Father!*"

"The people in the pub said he had children," she says, standing back and tilting her head to look at the stone. "And, look, underneath that..."

She's right. Now we've brought the letters to life there are more words emerging from the stubbly undergrowth. Together we claw the surface away, and then Florence runs over to the compost heap and comes back with a two-pronged garden fork.

"Should we do that? Aren't we, like, desecrating a grave?"

"Tidying it, more like," she says, plunging the

tines into the soil and scraping it back.

After a minute or so, we can see the stone properly. *"Father to Thomas, Derek and Sarah. Rest in Peace."*

"Thomas," I say. "Thomas who was caught up in the bullion robbery. The daughter moved away, that must be Sarah. And Derek — I wonder what happened to him?"

"Better put this back," says Florence, brandishing the fork before setting off over the lumpy, bumpy graves. I watch her running across to the shadowy heaps under the trees, and I'm sure that there's someone else here too. I just can't see them, but I can sort of feel them. I swing round quickly, wondering if I might catch sight of someone, and in the distance something moves under the big trees on the far side of the church. Perhaps it's just a cat but...

When she returns I ask, "Why do you think his grave hasn't collapsed? I mean, look at the others. They're all ... saggy. Do you think his coffin was made of stone or something?"

Florence walks up and down the row like she has any idea and then comes back and stands next to me. "Dunno," she says. "I agree, it's weird. But this churchyard is a bit weird. I mean, a bit creepy."

I'm glad I'm not the only one.

"Let's go," I say.

We exit, closing the tall scrapey gate that whines as it swings, as if no one's closed it for hundreds of years except for ghosts and skeletons.

I'm prickly hot, my palms sticky and my spine tingling, and I cling to the shade as we wander through the village. "We found Kenneth Fear's grave; we saw Mrs Barlow in her house. But I'm not sure we learned anything."

"Oh, we did," she says, counting on her fingers. "We know Mrs Barlow's husband disappeared in nineteen seventy-six. We know Kenneth Fear was buried in nineteen seventy-six. We know that he had three children, Thomas, Sarah and Derek. And that they must have lived in that house, right by the churchyard."

"True," I say, scratching the bite on my ankle. "And we know that Thomas went 'away' for twenty years. I think that means prison, for being involved in a bullion robbery."

"And moved 'up country'," she says. "Somewhere in the north, I'd bet."

We walk on.

"Which means that a load of gold disappeared at the same time as someone from the village disappeared. And that the car, which disappeared with the person that disappeared, has now appeared in the reservoir."

"There's no gold in that car," I say.

"No," she says. "Or anything else. Dunno – we might not see the significance of anything we know yet."

"What?"

"You know. Sometimes things just don't add up. D'you want to go swimming again?"

"Yeah," I say, wondering what on earth she means. "I totally do."

We grab Squish from the pub and almost run to the river. Crashing through branches, arriving at the bank we collapse in sweaty relief, half in, half out of the shade. I don't care this time and I jump in, shorts and T-shirt and all, and Florence follows. For ten glorious minutes we thrash the surface of the water, sending rainbow splashes up to the trees. Squish stands on the shore barking and dancing until he gives up and leaps in alongside, going from ball of fluff to curiously skinny dog.

He leaps out and shakes himself, spraying us both, but honestly I don't care – it's as if I've got my head back, my sense back, as if the cold water's shocked me awake.

"It's her husband," I say. "I'll swear he was in the car – so how did he vanish? Or how did what was left of him vanish?"

Florence pauses, submerging herself so that only her nose sticks over the surface, and then she talks in bubbles through the water before half choking and standing, laughing.

"You're right. And those scratches prove it. Someone took the body out."

"Body or bones," I say.

"Eeew!" says Florence. "I hope it was bones."

"So someone's hiding it."

"Or hiding the fact that it was there," she says.

"Not Mrs Barlow. She's too upset; she wants him back," I say, lying on my back and letting my feet float to the surface. I bounce gently down the stream, my bottom brushing the thick cushion of waterweed. This is so lovely; I could stay here forever.

"Definitely not," says Florence, pulling herself out of the water and jumping back in right next to my head so that I'm briefly swamped. "Right. Home."

And without warning she gets out of the river, squeezes the water out of her T-shirt and sets off for the village.

Chapter 7

I trot behind her, dripping and slowly heating up, but the deep chill of the river stays with me all the way home. Florence waves and runs off towards the pub, and I stop outside the cottage. The door's open, so I'm guessing that Mum's come back. It's kind of evening. The sun's definitely losing heat. Risking embarrassment, I peel off my shorts and T-shirt so that I'm standing there in my soggy underpants, and gently push the door open.

"Mum," I call. I can hear somebody moving around inside, but it sounds jerky. Flappy.

Stepping on to the mat I drop my clothes to the floor and peer round the door into the little sitting room. A mug lies on the floor. Cold tea spilling over the pristine white carpet. That doesn't look like the kind of thing Mum would do. As I stare, something crashes in the kitchen.

"Mum?" I call, and I step over the tea and into the kitchen. There's flour everywhere – or sugar, or both. It's all over the surfaces, all over the floor. I stop in the doorway. Broken glass covers the tiles. An empty green wine bottle and something clear, sticky. Elderflower cordial? Flowers and flower heads spill out from the sink, and the vase lies cracked in the washing-up bowl. The water has flooded into the sugar–flour mixture.

"Mum?" I say it quietly this time. Have we been burgled? Is this what burglars do? Were they searching for something?

I'm not sure I want whoever it is in the house to know I'm here. Grabbing my coat from where it's hanging on a hook in the hall, I pick my way round the broken glass and back towards the front door.

Crash.

Something goes over upstairs. If it's a burglar they're really noisy, and they don't care about getting caught.

Crash

Flapping. It's definitely flapping.

Flapping?

Holding the coat in front of me, like it's actually going to be any good in an emergency, I tiptoe to the bottom of the stairs.

"Hello!" I shout.

More crashing. More fluttering. It seems to be coming from my bedroom. I run up, bent over, ready to throw myself back down the stairs if I have to. The door to my room is half closed. For a moment I pause. Then, keeping low, I poke my head round the side to take a look. Something black whizzes towards me and I leap backwards, banging my head on the wall.

"Ow! What the—?"

It's a crow — a massive crow. Actually, not one but three and they seem to be destroying my room. The "Happy Place" cushion on the bed is covered in bird poo. The curtains are shredded and the bed full of feathers and bits and the crows seem really angry. So am I. Throwing the coat over my head I get round the far side of the bed and open the window before running back to the door and flapping the coat at the crows.

"Out!" I shout. "Go! Go! Fly away, you horrible things!" One of the birds hops to the frame and balances there for a moment before cawing and jumping off. As if connected, the second and third ones follow and the room falls suddenly silent.

I drop the coat in front of me and survey the damage. Epic. How could three small creatures do so much damage? How long have they been here?

I hear the door open downstairs.

"Dan! Dan! What the—"

We tidy. We sweat and we tidy and we make a collection of utterly broken things on the kitchen worktop. And then there's another pile of almost completely broken things. It's quite big.

"Three?" says Mum. "How could three of them get in? I mean, at once? That's really weird. Oh dear…" She dabs at some poo on a lampshade. "I don't think that's going to come off. That woman who owns the cottage'll be furious."

"There were definitely three," I say.

"But the door? Did I forget to lock it?"

"Dunno. It was definitely open. But even if you didn't lock it, you'd have shut it, and birds can't actually open doors, can they?"

I hold the dustpan as Mum sweeps the last flour drift into it. "I would have shut it, wouldn't I? My laptop and stuff's still here, so…"

I think back to the way I felt as I came in. "It was kind of frightening, Mum. Scary. I thought we'd been burgled."

She leans back against the counter, staring into the dustpan.

"Let's go and eat at the pub. I can't face cooking."

Although it's almost dark, we sit outside in the beer garden, which has a few lazy mozzies and a faint whiff of drains, and look through the menu. Normally I'd love to eat at the pub, but I'm all jumpy. I can't stop thinking about those crows flapping around the house. It was creepy. Horrible. And I can't help feeling stared at. I've felt stared at all afternoon. Ever since we went to Mrs Barlow's house. I try not to act self-conscious and self-consciously study the menu for too long. Then I read the fundraising flyer poked in next to the pepper on the table. *Fifty thousand pounds short of our target to renovate the village hall — all donations welcome.* Mum's distracted and gets into a long series of texts with Dave and Anya, before ordering fish and chips. I read the other side of the fundraising flyer. *The space is needed as a social venue for uniting the village. Knitting club, film club, Zumba, Scrabble — all ideas welcome.* Then Mum's phone rings and she goes off to have a conversation in the pub car park. I sit and stare at the sky losing its blue and turning midnight, and watch the bats swooping over the garden lights, snacking at speed. I want to know about the car and Mrs Barlow, and why she seemed scared of her own house, and whatever it was moving around in the churchyard earlier. I really want to know, but I also want to go home. Those birds.

I shudder.

This village is starting to get to me.

A bat skims past, steering between me and the glass in front of me.

My phone glows. It's Florence.

"*Look up!*" she texts, and I do. In a square of light up above the pub garden is a figure silhouetted at an open window.

"*Why are you here?*"

"*Something happened in our house. Crows.*"

"*What?*"

"*Birds — three birds.*"

I look at my phone but it doesn't glow and nothing comes back and then a waitress I haven't seen before comes out into the garden with the fish and chips and I sit, guarding them, blowing on a chip but not really feeling hungry.

My phone glows again.

"*Black birds in house mean death,*" says the message.

I look up at Florence's window but she's not visible.

"*Seriously?*" I type.

"*Seriously.*"

"*Superstition,*" I text back.

"*So?*" she says. "*Depends why they're there,*" she says.

Mum comes back clutching a bottle of ketchup and slapping at the air. "Mosquitoes," she says in explanation, and sprays herself with stuff from her handbag that settles on my food and tastes vaguely of soap.

"Mum," I say, scooping the peas off my plate and landing them on hers. "Florence says that a black bird in the house means death."

"Does she?" Mum picks the batter from her fish and begins to dissect the white flesh, one careful section at a time. "And do you believe her?"

"I don't know," I say, and I squeeze ketchup on to my plate.

An hour later we walk home. The air hums with heat and I begin to sweat even though it's dark. Unseen things rush past, brushing my skin. Probably biting it too. Everything feels awake, like nothing can sleep. The undergrowth rustles, and the scent of everything is amplified, from rose bushes to fox poo.

"Do you believe in the death-bird thing?" I ask Mum.

"No, of course not, but some people are superstitious and you kind of have to respect it. I vaguely remember your grandmother screeching when I put a new pair of trainers on the table. *No — new shoes on the table are very unlucky!*" she shouts in imitation of my grandma.

I laugh. "Yeah, but that's just rubbish. I mean, birds in houses must happen all the time. They wander in."

Mum goes silent for a while and we turn to walk along the wall by the church. Mrs Barlow's downstairs light is on and her curtains are drawn. Other windows are open, lights off, like gaping mouths and again the village feels creepy.

"There were three birds," she says to herself.

"Is that triply unlucky? Or..." I start, but I don't finish. What I'm thinking is that perhaps it means are we both going to die — and so's someone else?

We walk on through the balmy darkness, crunching unseen snail shells beneath our feet.

"No, I mean: how did three birds get in the house?"

She's right. It's been kind of bothering me. And then she starts talking. "Thing is, Dan, I'm digging up old graves. That's what I do all the time. A hundred years ago, I'd have had to do it at night or not at all. Remember all the stuff about Howard Carter digging up Tutankhamun? People thought the grave was cursed, and when the diggers died

81

of different things over the next few years, the superstitious ascribed those deaths to the curse of the tomb. So things have moved on. Even if your friend reads stuff into things that aren't real, you kind of have to respect that. But three birds at once... Maybe someone doesn't like me digging up the bones."

We're almost at the house when my phone buzzes. It's a message from Florence.

"Do you think the body could have fallen out of the car and be, like, at the bottom in the mud?"

Mum unlocks the door.

"I am so not going to look," I text, following her into the kitchen.

"Mum, after forty years, what would be left if there was a body in the lake? If it was a body I saw? What would be there? Gloop?"

Mum takes her phone out of her bag and puts it on charge. "Freshwater?" she says.

I nod.

"Bones. Just bones."

Chapter 8

It's another sweltering night, and I'm sure I don't really sleep. Strange sounds keep on crashing into my dreams – birds and owls and things scraping against the window – so that by five I'm wide awake. And I'm thinking about what Florence said.

Could there still be something or someone in the lake itself? If Laura's husband disappeared, and that's his car, then he might well be there too. He could have fallen out, but then the door would need to have been open and it wasn't. Also, nothing fell out of the car as it was towed from the lake.

Which means either he was a pile of bones at the bottom of the car, which the police would have noticed – or the big scratch on the door appeared overnight, and someone got to the car before the police did.

I'm thinking all this as I get dressed and slip out.

I'm not going to bother to leave Mum a note. I'll be back before she gets up.

If someone took him out of the car before the police arrived, they'd have had to have a vehicle. Surely?

There's a load of twittering outside the house and baby blue tits cascade out of the trees, dive-bombing me as I make my way round to the dam. No one else seems to be around yet, and there are cobwebs stretched over the lane, which catch in my hair and tug briefly before breaking.

Yuk.

The water in the dam has a thin layer of mist just above the surface and there are geese organising themselves into families and lining up to take off. It's damp, just like it was yesterday, which was why I wouldn't have noticed if anyone had been into the reservoir before I arrived.

The car is still there, towed up to the top of the ramp of mud, surrounded by police tape but unguarded.

I check. There's no one here, just a heron and the geese. And it's almost misty enough to give cover. Ducking under the tape, I walk over to the car and peer in through the partly open window. I thought there'd be some kind of layer filling the bottom, but someone's carefully removed it, and I can actually see the three metal sticks which must be all that's left of the foot pedals.

I try pulling at the door and it comes towards me surprisingly easily but it creaks as it opens. Crouching, I inspect everything I can see, which isn't much. The police must have taken everything out of the sides of the doors; they're empty. There's nothing under the seat except weed. No old parking tickets. Nothing. And it's beginning to smell mouldy.

I straighten up and walk round it. The outside is just as unhelpful. Except what's that?

I run my fingers over the windscreen. Is that a hole?

Sticking my head back inside the car I try to

manoeuvre myself into the driver's seat without actually sitting on it. There is. There's a hole, about the size of a coin, right in front of the driver. I poke my finger through it. Yes, it's definitely round. Definitely a hole.

At head height. Right between my eyes.

Backing out of the car, I take the fastest photo, stepping past the police tape and back over the soft mud away from the car.

A hole? At head height?

As fast as I can I text Florence and send the picture. She'll be fast asleep, but I want her to see it. See what she thinks. And then I wonder if the police saw it?

Did they even notice? It was quite hard to see, with the weed and the algae. Should I tell them?

I stop at the top of the bank and look down at the wet mud. Yesterday's footmarks are clear. And the tractor marks. They've got the chain caught up in them, and they cut deep. Idly I wander around thinking about the hole and gradually I realise that there are more marks. Another sort of vehicle. Something with tractor tyres but much smaller, and they go right up to the edge of the water. One of those little four-by-four things they use on farms? Something like that?

Again, I take pictures, and again, I send them to Florence. I'm not sure why but I want to make sure that if I lose my phone they don't disappear. That they'll be there if I need them.

Stopping to look across the reservoir I'm aware that I'm feeling watched again. But I can't be, can I? It could only be foxes or badgers at this time of day, surely.

I'm startled by a flight of geese taking off, almost laughing at the whomping noise their wings make and the full-on honk as they glide over my head. They've made me feel more normal and somehow braver. I could just follow those tracks. It wouldn't take a moment.

The lines run to the top of the bank, and then on into the baked grass. For a moment I think they've disappeared and then I see that they go off round the woods and that, like lines on a carpet, they've left a clear pair of tyre marks that run right over a field towards a gate on the far side.

I look around. Mum won't be up for at least another hour, and she'll probably think I'm still asleep. Breaking into the slowest run ever, I trot over the field, following the tracks to the boundary. The gate has huge wet pearl-necklace spiders' webs slung between the bars. I clamber over and stop in the lane. I realise that I don't really know where I am, and I pause, wondering whether to wander on up the lane or go back in the direction of the village. There's a farm up there, but then there are probably lots of farms around here.

Glancing back at the gateway, I can see that the vehicle I'm following must have turned right but nothing shows on the tarmac.

I'm still peering at the ground when a figure with a dog strides down the hill towards me. "Hello, Dan."

"Oh, Cat," I say. "Hello."

"You're up early. Couldn't sleep? Going to be another stinker, I think. What you looking at?"

I shake my head. "Nothing, really – just wandering, trying to work out things. You know." I'm aware I'm wittering, but she doesn't seem to mind.

She peers at where I've been looking. "Grass is dry," she says. "We need rain."

"Yeah." This is so awkward.

"Well, see you," she says. "Follow this road round; it'll take you back to the village. Gotta get back to the cows!" And she stomps off down the lane.

The clock in the village strikes six thirty, so I turn left and stroll uphill, the sweat already trickling down my back.

Once again I'm dive-bombed by baby blue tits threading back and forth in front of me, crossing and recrossing the tarmac. Ahead of me a dog barks in the village and behind a distant tractor starts its engine. Pausing at a wide patch of verge I look over the fields where the mist covers the tussocks.

I'm thinking.

Someone definitely drove something down to the water. Recently. Was it yesterday?

Standing on one leg, I pull strands of wet dead grass from my trainers. I'm still concentrating on this when I hear the roar of an engine behind me. There's plenty of room, I don't need to move, and I hear the tractor pass, hesitate, and then a second later, something makes me look up towards the sound of the engine.

It's carrying bales. Those big round bales covered in black plastic. And they're moving, sliding, slipping slowly from the back of the trailer. One bounces from the top of the pile and races off along the lane closely followed by another, which skims past me as it falls.

"Hey!" I shout. "Hey, your bales are getting loose! Watch out!"

I turn to the hedge. I can't get through it. There's barbed wire. Another bale rolls slowly towards me and I step aside, but I'm forced to scrabble up the verge. I'm going to have to get hold of the driver – or I'll be crushed.

"Hey! Help!" I shout again, jumping up and down and waving.

The bales shuffle on the trailer, some of the outer ones falling into the middle, and then three bales roll slowly from the back, filling the whole width of the lane, but moving, seriously moving. There's nowhere to go, and I turn and begin to trot back down the hill. Behind me the bales make a slick plastic sound on the road, almost silent but I can hear them, and as I run faster they roll faster.

It's a jog at first, a slow one, but soon I'm properly running, searching the hedgerow for a gap, but there aren't any, it's just the narrow lane, and the brambles reaching into it. The hill drops away getting suddenly steeper. I hadn't really noticed that on my way up.

I sprint, as hard as ever I've run, the air barely touching my lungs, my feet slapping on the ground. My trainers are too thin and it hurts – everything hurts. Behind me something squeaks, and perhaps one of the bales has stopped, or been stopped, but I can still hear the rolling, the slick sound, and then at last I can see the gate I came out of. Just down, just round the bend. Maybe two hundred metres of serious steep downhill. Reaching for more speed, stretching my legs, I hurtle along the last fifty metres, sweat pouring, feet pounding, skidding, sliding. The plastic of a bale bounces off my arm, not hard but far too close.

Thirty metres, twenty, ten, and I launch myself through the gate, a dive that ends in a messy skiddy somersault on the dry grass as the bales fly past, heading on down the lane.

I breathe.

Breathe so deep.
I stare at the sky.
And my heart hammers in my ears until I think it might explode.

Chapter 9

The engine roars somewhere up the hill. Things clank and bump.

What just happened?

Crawling up the field I tuck myself under the hedge, peering into the leaves. The tractor's turned round and is heading back down the lane, presumably in search of the missing bales. Brakes squeal, the trailer rattles. The tractor comes to a halt just by the gate.

Was that an accident? It didn't feel like it.

Fighting the urge to run, I pull my legs up

close and nestle right there in the roots of the scrubby shrubs that make up the hedge. Someone steps down from the tractor cab. They're wearing wellingtons. That's all I can see. I drag my legs right into my chest. The wellingtons stay put, then turn, then disappear back out on to the lane.

Down on the reservoir the last group of geese take off for their day's grazing.

I don't know how long I lie there on the scratchy grass taking huge gulps of air, waiting for my heart and my breathing to steady, but I'm aware that when I sit up the sun has risen and the geese have all gone.

With wobbling knees I stand to walk slowly down over the field towards the reservoir. Everything is shaky, my hands are shuddering, and when I try to get my phone out I drop it.

Stumbling, I get to the edge of the reservoir, and cross the dam, my legs feeling as if they belong to someone else. In the end I have to sit at the top of the steps and wait for my knees to firm up so that I can actually walk down the steep flight of steps rather than fall down it. From here I can hear the regular sounds of cars and people and dogs are getting going… Did that happen on purpose?

Gripping my wrists between my knees, I steady my hand enough to click the on button on the side of my phone. 6.55. Mum will still be asleep so I text Florence.

"*Nearly crushed by bales.*"

"*What?*"

"*Was checking car — something definitely been taken out of it.*"

"*Body?*" And then: "*Are you OK?*"

"*Just about.*"

"*How come bales?*" she asks.

"*Don't know,*" I reply.

"*Just seen the photos — holy smoke! Is that a bullet hole?*"

"*D'you think?*"

"*I'll come round now,*" she says.

Sitting on my trembling hands, I wait at the top of the steps watching the mist burn off the valley below and running the bales event over and over so that by the time Florence and Squish arrive, I'm absolutely sure it was deliberate.

"You'll have to tell the police," says Florence after I've told her. "That kind of thing doesn't happen by accident."

I nod. "But I've got to tell Mum first and she'll be furious."

"I could tell her?"

In the end we both walk back to the cottage and find that Mum's still fast asleep. I boil the kettle and stick some toast in the toaster. It feels surreal and I try really hard not to think about what could have happened. That squeak of plastic. They actually bumped into me — didn't they?

Mum thumps down the stairs to find me and Florence eating toast and marmalade up at the kitchen counter, talking about bones.

"What's happened?" she asks. "I can tell that something's happened. Tell me."

It's the same policeman. DC Boyle. The one with the wellingtons. He appears at the door, obviously hot and bothered, and even crosser when he sees me.

"What's all this then?" he says, taking out his notebook. "Someone said something about straw bales?"

"Just tell him, Dan," says Mum, and she checks

her phone for about the millionth time and types something in.

For a moment I wonder if I should just pretend it never happened.

"Um, yes," I say. "I'm – I was nearly squashed. If I hadn't been able to run faster than the bales, I would have been." I catch myself before I say it's deliberate. Somehow I don't think this is going to go down well with the policeman.

Mum looks over at him, and he puffs out his cheeks and lets out a long breath, making it quite clear that he either doesn't believe me or that he thinks this is a total waste of time. Or both.

"So you'd been at the reservoir?"

"Yes," I say.

"Did you see anyone there? Anyone to verify your story?"

He doesn't believe me and then I remember Cat. "Yes, Cat, she saw me. We spoke."

"Catherine Fowler?"

I look at Mum, she shrugs. "S'pose so," I say. "I don't actually know her name."

"But was she there when the bales were falling off the trailer?" he asks.

I shake my head. "No, she'd gone off down the lane. She was walking her dog."

"OK, I'll talk to her, see if she's any idea whose tractor it might have been. Now, why were you at the reservoir?"

Florence clears her throat and I look up to see her glaring.

"Had you gone to take another look at the car, perhaps?"

Almost without moving, Florence shakes her head. I think about the hole in the windscreen. Mum'll hate the sound of that.

"Um, not really..." I tail off.

Now all three of them are staring at me.

"I mean, I wasn't near it. I didn't touch it." I feel the blush fill my ears and wonder if Mum spots it. "I was just enjoying the early-morning cold. The birds and..."

Mum turns to the policeman; she has spotted my ears. "He's lying," she says. "I can always tell when he's lying. His ears go red."

"Mum!" I say. "That's not fair. Yes, OK, I did go to the car – but I didn't do anything, except follow some tracks that went up the hill behind."

"What kind of tracks?" says the policeman.

"Something, or someone, came down to the car in a small truck or tractor before the big tractor pulled the car out of the lake yesterday," I say. "I found the tracks this morning."

The policeman narrows his eyes and looks sideways at me. "How d'you know it's before?"

"Because the big tractor tyre marks go right through them," I say, getting my phone out and flicking through until I find the picture of the tyre marks. "See. The tractor tyres have left big dents in the smaller track."

He peers at my phone. "Could have been weeks ago."

"The grass is flattened," I say.

"Quite the investigator, your boy," the policeman says to Mum.

She nods. "Reads too many mysteries," she says. "But... the bales?"

Stretching his legs, DC Boyle tilts his head from side to side. "Might be nothing. Either way, you're getting a bit of a reputation, young man. I'd recommend staying in with a murder mystery on the telly – keep out of trouble."

Florence squeaks and I glance over to see that she's holding her hands over her mouth and that her eyes and forehead are set into a ferocious scowl.

"I'll keep him with me today," says Mum. "Had a bit of a shock, so you can come and scrape old bones with me and the team, Dan. No body-searching today." She glances at Florence. "Which probably means the same for you too."

I sense that Mum doesn't really know what to make of Florence. She appears to have no boundaries, or at least her grandfather is so busy that he never follows her, or gets cross or anything, but I know Florence's mum texts her all the time, so she's still on a leash – just a really long one compared to mine.

"I'll be off then," says DC Boyle, raising his arms to stretch and showing us all two dark sweat circles under his armpits. "Will pop over and see if anyone's missing a bale or two."

"And will you tell us what you find?" asks Mum.

"Due course, due course. I'll let myself out," he says.

She goes to the door with him, and Florence and

I sit on the white sofas in silence.

In the end she opens her mouth to speak and then closes it again. "I've been thinking about what you said about the windscreen and the tracks and all of it – and I think someone HAS to have taken the body out of the car before the police turned up. They took it and hid it."

"But it would just be bones," I say.

"Yeah, but those bones must be able to tell a story. Like when your mum digs up some ancient body and finds out that they died of – I don't know, poisoning or something. She can do that, right?"

"I can, yes," says Mum, coming back into the room. "But you two have done enough of this. I'm really not having it. I've a job to do, and, yes, I know it's the summer holidays, but you're seriously getting in my way, AND you're wasting police time. Whatever the reason for the car in the lake, it isn't your business." She sounds pretty calm, but I can hear the fury underneath. "I think – just as the constable thinks – that you should confine yourselves to fictional mystery. Watch *Murder, She Wrote* or something. If there's really something going on, let the police find out. Don't get in their way. It's really irresponsible."

I glance at Florence. She's looking at the floor, like people do when they're being told off and don't want to cry. If I argue, Mum'll lay it on thicker, and although I'm fairly used to it I don't think Florence would like Mum in full fury mode. It's not pretty.

"OK," I say. "But can we still wander around? I mean, go swimming and that kind of thing?"

Mum looks to me and then to Florence. Florence pulls a full puppy face and miraculously manages to look like the cutest little six-year-old with her feet dangling from the sofa and her eyes all wide and hurt.

"Gosh," says Mum, coughing. "Well, I suppose you can roam, but no poking around. No investigating, and that is only if Florence's parents will be happy with the idea of you two still hanging out together."

Florence nods, keeping her eyes in full puppy. "Granddad won't mind. My parents aren't here."

The corner of her mouth quivers with what might be a sob – or it might be a giggle.

"Right, you can roam later, but for now, Dan,

you're staying with me," says Mum, sniffing. "Now that half the day's gone, I really must go and do some work. You're welcome to come up and join us later, Florence. We'll have lunch in the shade, probably about twoish. OK?" Mum gives Florence the kind of look that says get lost right now.

In silence Florence slips out of the door and I wait about three minutes before my phone begins to vibrate with texts.

"*Must find body,*" she says.

"*Yes, but Mum,*" I reply.

"*Will bring Squish for a walk. Can take him off into the woods.*"

"*See you later,*" I text, hoping that Mum won't be keeping too close an eye on me.

Chapter 10

Part of me wants to go back to bed and stream a movie. Actually quite a big part but I can't. I have to go and meet Florence and somehow we're going to have to see if we can find some evidence. If the birds and the bales were deliberate, then someone is trying to frighten us off – or frighten me off. If they're trying to frighten Florence off, it would be harder; she lives in the pub. Her granddad's like a bear guarding the door. Mum and I are out here on our own.

I shudder.

Didn't Mrs Barlow tell us to be careful? But we should absolutely not stop. And if someone wants to frighten us away, then all the more reason to find out.

I tell myself all this in front of the mirror and strike various punchy poses, trying to look bigger, older and stronger than I am, sticking the scared Dan deep down at the bottom of my toes. But the scared Dan is still in my eyes. The scared Dan is thinking of huge plastic bales bounding down the road, of birds flapping and of eyes watching from the shadows. I harden my focus, but I can still see him. This is no good; I don't want Florence to see him – I'll have to try to keep him hidden.

I follow Mum through the baking heat past an orchard where blood-coloured mulberries have splatted in the grass and there's the buzz of drunken wasps, and it occurs to me that Mrs Barlow might have taken the body. And then I think about her all bent over and sad and I can't see her wading across the lake in the dark to dig bones out of a car. I can't imagine her even managing to open the door of the car.

No, that's silly. She didn't. She even asked us if we were sure we'd seen him in there. I look around to see if she's waiting up on the dam, but there's no sign of her and I realise that I haven't seen her since she was in her garden.

"Now, you don't have to dig. You can go up and sit in the shade," says Mum. "Keep cool for now."

She heads for the sweltering white gazebo that's protecting all the diggers and I wander up the bank and crunch over the undergrowth to sit on a shady tussock. Behind me something rustles and a nose emerges, followed by the rest of Squish.

"Hello, Squish," I say.

"Shh," says Florence's voice from a bush.

"Hello, Florence," I say.

"Don't look at me," she says.

"What, in case Mum's watching?" I ask. "She can't see up here."

"Perfect," says Florence. "We can get going, start searching. I reckon it'll be in a barn somewhere. Someone will have hidden the bones in their compost heap or something."

"There's miles of farmland here – they could be anywhere."

I can practically hear the cogs of Florence's brain working.

"They wouldn't have had long. And they might be worried about getting caught. They probably wouldn't hide them in their house, or bury them in their own garden, because that's the first place someone would look if they suspected someone."

"So they've hidden it somewhere public?"

"Yeah, but not the middle of the village — it would be too obvious."

"You realise that the whole of a skeleton would probably fit in a large carrier bag," I say, looking down at the diggers scraping earth from the ancient bones beneath. "Although the skull's quite heavy and the leg bones — femurs — can be quite long."

"Yuk, Daniel — how would you even know that?"

"I've spent my whole life living with old bones."

It's Squish that finds the bones.

"Today is going to be epically hot," says Florence as we head over to the swimming spot, sweat stinging the corners of my eyes. As we walk, I text Mum to tell her where I am. I notice Florence's doing the same. But honestly I'd go swimming even if Mum said no – it's just unbearable today. Mum texts back a series of cross emojis but at least emojis are better than furious language.

I text back a string of hearts.

She sends me a kiss.

"We'll go further up. I bet Emma and yukky Adam will be at the swimming hole, and I don't want to see them snogging. The other one has a big tree with roots that go down to the water. I don't think we're supposed to swim there, but, hey, who's going to know?"

Off the path we usually use is a little break in the undergrowth. It might be a badger run and Florence heads that way. We reach the river and pick our way along another almost-path. On the other side is farmland, cows flicking flies with their tails, sheep clustering in the shade. Everything's buzzing with the heat and I'm as uncomfortable as I've ever been. Wearing my swimming trunks under my shorts is making this super-sweaty.

"Not much further," she says.

We reach the stubbly grass by the side of the river and kick off our shoes. Within a minute we're swinging into the water on creepers and vines. It's freezing, wonderful. Arcs of water form rainbows and Squish stands on the shore barking at us, leaping in the spray, until he too gives up and plunges into the water.

"Oh, Squish!" shouts Florence, beating him back. He claws his way up the bank and shakes himself dry before flying through the air again to land upstream.

This time I'm actually going to swim, and I lean back, feeling the intense cold on the back of my head, swinging my arms into backstroke and my legs so that they kick the clear water high into the overhanging trees. It only takes a moment to cross the river and I crash into the muddy shallows on the far side, which have been trampled by cows leaving green pockets of stagnant water.

"Eeew!" I stand, and the mud squishes between my toes and sucks at my feet. "Urgh!"

"Jump in again!" Florence yells, floating in the middle of the deepest part.

Holding my nose, I stagger over the cow-pocked mud up on to the grassy bank and leap again, landing in the water right next to Florence, drenching her and shooting water up over both banks.

"Yay!" I shout.

"That's so mean!" shouts Florence, and Squish paddles past us to investigate something under the water.

While Florence clambers out, to jump in again, I try swimming on my front, but my knees tangle in the weed and I remember that rivers have eels and go back to leaping about and swimming on my back.

Squish is tussling with the river bed, and eventually turns to face me, with something in his mouth.

"What have you got, Squish?"

It looks like a brown ball. A large brown ball with a lump on one side that's gripped between Squish's teeth.

"Come here, boy," I say, but he heads for Florence up on the bank and scrambles over the tree roots to stand by her side, dropping his find by her feet before shaking himself violently.

Avoiding the spray, Florence leans over to peer at Squish's find, while alongside her, Squish smiles. That is, if a dog can smile. I plough back across the river, clunking into the far side and turning round.

Up on the bank Florence's face goes from curiosity to horror to delight.

"What is that? Oh!" she shouts. "Oh no! Dan! Look! Squish, you clever dog. He's found a skull!"

"For real?" Splashing to the side I take a good look at the object from ground level.

"Look, see." Florence reaches forward to turn it.

"No, don't touch!" I say. "Use a stick or something. They'll want to dust it for fingerprints."

Florence raises her eyebrows. "It's been in Squish's mouth. I mean, a dog's mouth and the bottom of the river. It's our body, isn't it? From the car? Must be."

"Still, I don't think you should touch it." From where I'm standing it looks like half a skull, with the jaw missing. And there's a hole in the side of it, which might be from Squish's teeth. It's brown, dark brown, like it's been stained with tea for the last fifty years, but it doesn't look like the ones Mum digs up – it looks harder. Newer.

"I'll call the police," says Florence, crouching. "Tell them we found the body."

As she dials, I haul myself out of the water. It suddenly seems far less attractive. I think I'd rather be hot than swim in a river full of human bones. Squish leaps in again, and this time he stays on the surface. Part of me wants him to dive under and see what else he can find. Part of me would rather he didn't.

Water pools around my feet and I squat over the skull. The hole is round – very much like Squish's tooth. It doesn't look that fresh, but then what do I know about these things? I take my phone from where I jammed it in a tree and take a load of pictures. Especially of the hole.

Florence's still on the phone, looking away.

I poke my little finger through the hole. It fits. Just like the hole in the windscreen.

"Wait with it? Here? But how long are you going...? Well, OK, I guess, but the dog's going to need feeding. And I'm—" She stands up and swings her head between her knees, bringing it up fast so that her braids flick water all over me and the trees.

"Hey!" I say, wiping the water off my screen.

"Sorry," she says. "It was just in the river – the dog got it out. No, I can't see..." She leans forward, balanced on her toes, staring into the river. "I can't – I mean, there might be more. Do you want us to look?" She pulls her face into something approaching disgust. "No – OK – you've got my number an' that." She nods her head repeatedly and then puts the phone down.

"And?" I say.

"And they'll come."

"When?" I say, using a stick to tip the skull upside down.

She shrugs. "Dunno. Soon."

"I'm just gonna take a few more pics."

Chapter 11

I text Mum. In an attempt to avoid a howler I just say we've made a discovery and that we're by the river. I send her the map coordinates to make her feel better, and she sounds quite calm when she rings me back. "We're just having a break. Don't you two want some food?"

"Um, we're OK for now. Save us something," I say. Luckily she can't see my ears turning red.

It's the first policeman again – the one who came when we spotted the car. He calls to us through the bushes and when he arrives he's practically melted and his hair is full of mossy twigs. "What is it this time – the report mentioned a skull?"

Florence stands back and points, and I'm massively happy to see that his eyes practically pop out of his head when he sees that it's a real human skull. He doesn't talk to us at all. Instead he gets someone on the phone.

"SOCOs, now," he says, reading out the coordinates and wandering away into the undergrowth so that I can only hear odd words. "Kids … find … river … dog."

And then we answer all the questions all over again and it's his turn to peer into the water.

"Do you think there are more in there?" he asks.

"We could send Squish in to search," Florence says.

"I don't think that's a good idea," says the policeman, answering his phone. "Yes, no, yes, two minors found it. Yes – they seem OK, actually." He looks at us both. "Counselling?"

I shake my head. "I'm used to bones," I say.

"So am I," says Florence, lying. "Is it the body from the car?"

The policeman glares at her and turns his back.

"Let's go," I say. "While he's on the phone."

We wave goodbye to his back and head along the badger path, until his voice has merged with the birdsong and all we can hear is splashing and high-pitched laughter further ahead. Squish trots off through the undergrowth to investigate.

"Emma and Adam," says Florence. "I wonder if they know they're swimming in bone water."

We crash on, heating up much faster than I'd hoped, until we can see the gazebo and the reservoir and Mum, who looks far too hot.

She sits back on the burned grass and swipes her forehead, leaving earth sticking to the sweat. "How was your swim? Talk me through the freezing-cold water bit."

I glance at Florence. She nods.

"We found the bones. Or, at least, we found some bones."

Mum narrows her eyes and looks at each of us in turn. "Bones? Is this that wretched car again?"

"We don't know for sure," says Florence. "But show her the pictures, Dan."

Mum squints at my phone. "I can't really see, but this looks like a male skull. Although ... what's that on the top?"

Squatting down next to Mum I enlarge the screen. "It's a hole. It could have been Squish, though – he was the one who found it; he grabbed it and took it out of the river and dumped it next to Florence."

"Like a present," says Florence.

"Nice," says Mum. "I can't tell – I'll have a look at home, but…" She shrugs. "Old bones, old bones…"

"We just went swimming," I say. "Really, we didn't mean to find anything—"

"Hmm," says Mum. Standing up, she brushes dead grass from the back of her legs. "I wanted to go to the museum, but I'm guessing the police will want to ask you more questions, so we might have to stay here."

On cue, Mum's phone rings. It's the police. It's like they've got her on speed dial.

"Could you talk to him this evening? It's just that I need—" Her face creases as if she can hardly hear the person on the other end. "No – I need to go to the museum – yes – about sevenish?" A long trail of sweat runs through the dust on her legs. "Why not?" she says. "Well, I'm sorry, but you can't come now – you're going to have to wait." She takes the phone from her ear and stabs at the buttons until it stops bleating.

"Right," she says, smiling a tight smile. "Let's go to the museum. Florence, what are you doing now?"

"You've got the eye sockets and the cranium, but no teeth," says Mum, struggling with the gear stick of our hire car. I don't think she even knows she said it aloud, so I keep quiet, listening.

Finally getting into first gear, we lurch out of the tiny parking space next to the cottage and into the lane, which has suddenly become much narrower since Mum got behind the wheel.

"But that could just be the dog," she mutters. "Or the river."

"I'm guessing that someone threw the whole lot in the river thinking it would never be found," I say. "But we happened to find it."

Mum doesn't speak, so I go on.

"Florence said no one ever goes there, and no one had been there for a while, because it was all overgrown…" As I say it I realise that the bones would have had to have been thrown in from the other side of the river, the bit where the cows were. No one could possibly have been along that path. Otherwise we'd have found it easier to get through.

"You shouldn't even be thinking about it," says Mum, letting out a little yelp as she skims past a tall wall and just avoids a white van hurtling towards us. "Leave the police to work it out."

We arrive at the museum, which does have air conditioning, and Mum goes off to talk to someone about the dig. I wander through the huge empty spaces, looking at pictures of dead people, and dead things, and get to drink hot chocolate and eat biscuits with Mum and a nice man called Jonathan, who runs the place and who has secret drawer after secret drawer of things that have been dug up.

"And this is the necklace that we found before we found the site you're working on," he says, taking some beads from a box padded with cotton-woolly stuff. "Lapis and turquoise," he says.

"And is that gold?" I ask, pointing at something extraordinarily shiny and modern.

"Yup." He nods his head. "So the bones belong

to a woman of some importance," he says. "But not necessarily Edith. We just need something more to prove it's her."

Mum's frantically taking photos and tapping notes into her phone. "Exciting, isn't it, Dan? Edith was married to Harold – King Harold – but after Hastings she disappeared. To think this could be her!"

Today feels really weird. Like when you're ill at school and your mum comes in and takes you out, but she's got a whole load of stuff planned so you end up eating chips in a garden centre with one of her friends and kind of wishing that every day could be like that. Not that I'm eating chips, or in a garden centre, but I like museums. And I like being with Mum, and I love to see her happy and excited.

"I'm hoping the call with Copenhagen can help us with that," says Jonathan. "Apparently they have a lead on the necklace."

"We're going to do a conference call with them," says Mum, "so you'll have to be really quiet for a bit. OK, Dan darling?"

I look around the office. It's full of filing cabinets

and boxes and I have an idea. "Can I look in the old newspapers?" I ask Jonathan.

"Of course," he says, and he takes me through a side door to a large cupboard that contains a dusty desk, a huge bank of wooden drawers and a grey machine that looks like an ancient computer, but not quite. "They're supposed to be being put on digital, but we haven't got the funding. If you can work it out, you can access everything through this." He shows me all the boxes of film, organised by newspaper and date, and also how the machine works. Leaving the door open, he goes back into the main office with Mum. They settle in a corner and soon they begin talking to someone miles away.

I find nineteen seventy-six and after I've looked at lots of wedding photos and reports of missing bins, I begin to get the hang of the local papers. *The Herald* is the one with all the sensational news. *The Chronicle* has loads of advertisements for horseboxes and dog beds, but seems to report things with smaller headlines. On the whole I think I believe in *The Chronicle* more. Among the death notices in early July nineteen seventy-six I find Kenneth Fear. It doesn't say much. Just *No flowers* and *Mourned by*

Sarah, Derek and Thomas. Burial at St Thomas' Church, 2.30 Friday 16th. So I've found the right time.

I scroll through more reports from the same month. Lots of adverts, a big article about the drought, and pictures of the reservoir. Empty but nothing like as empty as it is now. So the car could have gone in then and disappeared.

I lift out the second week of July sheet from the box and slide it under the viewer, but this isn't the same. I scroll up to the top and see that it's a national paper that strayed into the local collection. I'm about to take it out when I spot a headline.

1st July 1976 – Bullion theft, Heathrow Airport. An estimated three and a half million pounds' worth of gold bullion was stolen from a secure warehouse in Hayes, Middlesex, in the early hours of yesterday morning. Police are searching for a blue Ford in connection with the theft. A security guard was left with life-threatening injuries but is said to be in a stable condition in hospital.

Blue Ford?

That's it. That has to be the same car. We have a blue Ford in the lake. So Mrs Barlow's husband was driving a car that was involved in the robbery. And if the bones we found are his, he ended up with a hole in his head.

A shiver goes down my spine.

Be careful, she said.

I look up at the clock. I don't have long. They've already been on the phone for ten minutes. Frantically I check through the next few sheets mostly looking for mentions of a missing person, but I can't find any. There are also some sheets missing; they could easily have got muddled up. I glance up at the hundreds of boxes arranged neatly to my left. They could be anywhere.

Going through the ones I have, I find more pictures of the drought, and people talking about stand pipes and the government being to blame for not planning. No mention of global warming. Perhaps they didn't know about it?

I pull out the next sheet from the box. *The Chronicle*. Second week of July. More drought, more weddings, more horses for sale. Lots of mentions of heatwaves, and hosepipe restrictions, again talk of the reservoir being low, suggestions that water tankers would have to come in. Then there's a picture of the pub with lots of people outside holding up pint glasses because they'd raised enough money to buy a new roof for the village hall. The same roof that is being replaced now.

On the next sheet I find:

Sandford — The burial of one of the liveliest figures of the village. Kenneth Fear was known for his entertaining stories and endless local knowledge. He was seen off by a large number of local residents and two of his three children, Sarah and Thomas.

Two?

Where was the third?

Thomas was about to be arrested, but he made it to his father's funeral. Derek didn't — why not?

Rubbing my eyes I tidy up the sheets and put them back in the boxes. I put the national one back where it should be and find another copy of *The Chronicle* in that box. Someone must have muddled them.

Mum and Jonathan are still talking to the person in wherever it is, so I put the stray sheet under the viewer.

More drought. More pictures of fêtes and children and dogs. Then:

Sandford — Local man arrested over Hayes bullion robbery.

Twenty-four-year old Thomas Fear has been charged with multiple offences relating to the 1st July Hayes bullion robbery. In a statement Police Constable Amos Short stated that Fear wasn't the only person involved, and that they had more leads to follow. However, he has been positively identified by the security guard. The Metropolitan Police are appealing for more information.

So Thomas Fear's dad died more or less when he was actually carrying out a robbery. Then he goes back to Sandford, buries his dad and is arrested a few days later?

Twenty years they said. That would be nineteen ninety-six. He'd be out by now. Where did he go afterwards?

And did they ever find the gold?

I reach for my phone and try to raise Google. Nothing. No signal.

"Dan?" Mum's voice. "Dan, darling — we can go back now."

"OK." As I close down the machine and put the microfiche slides back in their boxes I struggle to write a text to Florence. It'll go out when we leave, although I'm on three per cent charge and it says it's going into emergency mode.

Chapter 12

We step out of the door into incredible heat. The tarmac hasn't actually melted but it's so hot it burns my feet through the soles of my shoes and instantly sucks all the moisture out of my mouth. The car's baking, the seats are sauna hot, and Mum winces when she grips the steering wheel. Jonathan waves us off and we roll slowly down the road from the museum with all the windows open, until the heat in the car goes from volcanic to desert.

"Brilliant," says Mum. "That was brilliant – so much information. And the really exciting thing is that the necklace is almost certainly Danish. We could really have found her, Dan. Jonathan's sending them photos to compare to other necklaces they've found. And they reckon the age is right. A woman in her sixties. That's quite old for the eleventh century."

"Good," I say, thinking about what I found out and wishing I'd been able to discover more. I could have looked at later copies of the papers to see if there was anything about the other two siblings. They might still be around. Sarah Fear might have married someone locally, and there'd be a wedding notice. How annoying – I didn't even think of that. As Mum chats I stare out of the window at people's dry gardens, children playing in paddling pools, dead grass lining the road.

I try to make everything I know add up.

I can't quite see the connections, but the coincidences are too massive to ignore.

First: Mrs Barlow's husband disappeared just when they buried Kenneth Fear.

Second: Thomas Fear was involved in the bullion robbery.

Third: there's a car with a hole in the windscreen,

and a skull with a hole.

And then there are the crows, and the bales, and someone moving the bones. Although all of it happened a really long time ago, the car has triggered something more recent. So someone's still around. Who?

Thomas?

But people in the village would have seen him. Someone would recognise him. And why? Why would he still be here?

We leave the town and drive through dry yellow fields with green trees lining their borders.

"All right?" says Mum. "How are you feeling? What a day!"

"I'm—"

She slams the brakes on and the car slews to a halt, nearly in the hedge. In front of us is an ambulance and a huge leaf-covered tree blocking the road.

"What the—"

A fire engine screeches to a halt behind us, and six people wearing heavy yellow jackets rush out and swarm around the ambulance. On the far side a police car has stopped with lights flashing and there are a couple of cars. Two of the firefighters run back to the engine and emerge with a chainsaw and another machine.

"Oh no," says Mum. "Funny time of year to have a tree down – perhaps it's the drought. Stay here, Dan. I'll go and see if I can help move anything."

I watch as she skirts the ambulance and stops. I can't see what she sees but I can guess. She holds her hand up to her mouth and turns away, horrified.

"Mum?" I half open the door.

"Stay where you are," she calls, and then she talks to someone before coming back to the car and climbing into the driver's seat.

"What is it? What's happened?" I ask.

"Some poor person – I don't know who – caught in their car, under..."

She doesn't need to say more.

We sit in our car, sweating in full sunshine, Mum periodically glancing at her phone, me wishing I'd charged mine. I don't know if the message I sent will have reached Florence.

After about ten minutes, Mum tries to turn the car round, but there are too many cars behind us to move and she gives up, leaving us jammed half across the road. We get out and sit in a tiny patch of shade on the verge.

"Do you think I could just walk to the village?" I ask.

"Stay here, Dan. I think you'd just get in the way."

There's shouting and the sound of chainsaws, and chunks of tree appear in the field alongside, dragged there by the sweating firemen.

Another fire engine arrives, followed by a crane on a low-loader, and Mum gets back in our car and drives it into the hedge so that the crane can get past. She gets out and joins me again.

We had one bottle of water between us. "You drink it, Dan," says Mum, pointing at the last feeble drop and gazing longingly towards the river. I look where she's looking. There's a field with a few bushes in it and a kind of ditch that runs straight towards the river. Cows have clustered by the fence and are eyeing the activity with a mix of fear and curiosity, blowing the flies that land on their noses into small buzzing clouds that drift over our heads.

On the far bank are trees and a thicket of smaller trees, and as I stare I realise that the blue flowers I can see in the hedge are actually scraps of police tape. Mum's busy on the phone to Cat so I wander over to the car, open the door and clamber on to the ledge to give myself another few centimetres. It is. It's the place where we found the bones this morning, but this time from the other side of the field. There's some blue police tape strung round the trees and now I can see a man in waders in the river and a woman on the bank in a white suit. At least they're taking the bones seriously.

Shadows are starting to stretch across the road, and the light's turning yellow. A vast tree trunk lifts from the ground and swings over into a field and the sound of mechanical metal cutting crescendoes. Minutes later, the blue light switches on on top of the ambulance and the engine starts. As it weaves its way through the fire engines and parked cars, a mangled heap of car and windscreen and seat stuffing is whisked high in the air and dumped on the side of the road. Someone starts to brush the glass together and the drivers from either side mutter to each other. Other people arrive on foot and on bicycles. Some of the diggers, the people from the post office, Uncle Tony with Aimee, the waitress from the pub, Cat, some of the chin-strokers from the dam. Florence's granddad arrives, and I can see he looks very worried, asking the police and firefighters lots of questions. He keeps on looking back towards the village and then he makes a long phone call to someone. Then, as if it's all over, everyone clambers back into their cars and we're waved through a sandy, oily puddle and off towards the village. As we pass the tree stump I'm amazed to see that the whole thing seems to have come out of the ground in one go. Uprooted. Almost as if it was pushed.

"That's weird," I comment, but Mum doesn't say a word until we get back to the cottage.

"I'll make pasta," she says, sagging on to a stool in the kitchen.

"OK." I run up the stairs and hear the rumble of her voice through the floor. She's obviously trying to keep her voice down, but for once I'm not going to listen in. Fumbling by my bed I find my charger and wait for the battery to creep into life. It's so slow, and slower if I watch, so I take myself to the window and witness the first mosquitoes bloom from the trees, and the first bats come out to eat them. The blue of the sky deepens and the leaves at the very top of the tree are all that's left of the sun's rays.

I turn back to my phone. Ten per cent. That's enough, isn't it?

As the screen flips into life, I think about all the things I want to tell Florence. But it's her messages to me that cascade through in a long procession of buzzes before I've even tapped out the first text.

"Guess what!"

"Hellooo!"

"Dan?"

"Helloooo!"

"You there?"

"Dan!!"

"You gotta ring me!"

"You OK?"

"Dan."

"Dan"

"Dan — Where are you?"

"Have you heard about the tree?"

Her last message is from about five minutes ago.

I text back. *"Yes — I saw it. We were stuck for a while. Sorry, phone battery flat."*

"It was Laura Barlow in the car."

I read the words over and over. Mrs Barlow?

"That's awful." It's not really what I mean but I can't think how to say it. It's not like I know her, but I have spoken to her and she was so sad last time we saw her. *"How do you know?"*

"Granddad saw it — he rang me. And I'm not allowed out! Emma is but I'm not!"

She sends me a string of emojis that don't work on my phone, but might be something with its tongue stuck out. A car draws up in the lane. It's a police car.

Our doorbell rings.

"Did you get my text? From earlier?" I say.

"No. What did it say?"

"Dan! Dan! Come here!!!" Mum calls up the stairs.

I fumble with the phone and give up. It'll wait.

We get new police. Ones I haven't met before and who don't seem to know anything about anything, so I have to go back to explaining the car in the reservoir and the towing and the tractor and the missing body, and Laura Barlow looking so upset.

"But these bones?" says the man. He's tall and red-headed and has sunburn on the side of his neck. He's not wearing a uniform. The woman with him is short and dark-haired with shining black eyes that remind me of a field mouse. Seeing everything. Missing nothing.

Mum stands in the doorway watching, but she doesn't say anything.

"So we went swimming."

"Can you show us on this map?" The woman holds up a tablet and shows me a satellite view of the reservoir. Funny, I'd not realised how big it is from the air. It goes back miles and it takes me a while to work out where the first swimming place is.

"So we didn't go here, because of Emma and Adam."

"Who are they?" asks the woman. "Friends of yours?"

I glance up to see Mum raising her eyebrows. "Emma is Florence's sister, and Adam's her boyfriend."

"So you went somewhere else?"

"Yes, here, I think." I point further up the river.

It's fatter and I think it's probably where we were, but I'm not sure why I'm showing her, because they already know that's where we were. As I examine the map, I see the tree still standing and the farmland spreading around the river on all sides.

"So what happened? How did you find the bones?"

I'm sure they must know it was Squish but I tell them anyway. "And so he just dumped it on the side of the river."

"And you didn't touch it?"

I shake my head.

"Or move it?"

I hesitate and then shake my head and I feel the tips of my ears heat up.

Mum lowers her head and stares at me.

I shake my head again.

"So neither of you moved it, or prodded it, or touched it?"

"No," I say, horribly conscious of the colour of my ears.

There's some writing and some sighs and some tapping of stuff into phones.

"Is it the body from the lake?" I ask.

"What do you know about that?" the policeman asks, resting his hand on the burned skin on the back of his neck.

"I don't — I mean, I don't know if there was a body, but Mrs Barlow seemed to think there ought to be, so..."

"Well, thank you very much," says the man, standing up.

"Yup. Very helpful," says the woman.

"Good," says Mum. "Glad he could help. Now..." She indicates the doorway and gently ushers the pair of them out of the house.

And then she sits down and looks at me.

"Tell me, Dan. Tell me everything."

Chapter 13

I don't. Of course I don't. She'd be so worried ... and I'm not sure – it doesn't all fit. Yet.

I mean, she knows about the bales. And the bones, and the car. But I don't tell her about the gold bullion robbery, or the Fears, or the fact that there were three children. One of them went to prison, but there's no trace of the other two. And that it has to somehow be connected. Although...

"Hmmm." She sits back, hardly visible in the mosquito dark. She's quiet for a long time and then goes into the kitchen to finish cooking.

She doesn't turn on the radio, or sing, or do anything noisy. She's just quiet.

I nip upstairs to message Florence. Surprisingly there are no messages from her.

"Food!" shouts Mum up the stairs.

"For once, I'm laying down the law," she says, mopping a sea of boiled pasta water from the stove top. "I need to know where you are. Not that I'm being a helicopter parent, but I'm worried about everything that keeps on happening. I mean, poor Mrs Barlow. How awful. I can't help wondering how long she was there for before anybody found her. And that skull ... and, honestly, I'm not sure I can stand the sight of another policeman. Let's just let everything calm down, eh?"

There's no point arguing. I'll wait. Mum'll soften, but actually I'm quite glad she's keeping me near her. Every time I close my eyes I can see the bales falling from the trailer or the tree across the road and it makes me feel sick.

We eat pasta with the telly on, and there's a reporter "at the scene" who interviews the fire service and a police constable and they appeal for witnesses, and show a picture of a devastated farmer who said he thought his tree was sound, and then they don't say any more.

"But how is the poor woman?" Mum asks the telly as the story moves to planning extensions to a golf club somewhere on the other side of the county.

"Mum, can I borrow your laptop? Just to check something?"

"Course," she says from the sofa.

I sit at the table, facing Mum, my back to the wall. On her computer she has access to a library of skulls. Don't all parents have access to a library of skulls?

I search for ones with holes in. Most of Mum's favourites are ancient, so the holes are from pickaxes and swords, but there's a whole load labelled GSW. Gunshot wounds.

I run upstairs to get my phone. It's half charged, and I fire up the pictures I took by the river as I skate down the stairs.

I look at the skull, and the cracks around it, and then I skim through the pictures on the computer. Until I find one.

The picture is of a skull, white, with a hole,

ragged on one side, neat on the other. Apart from the colour of the bone, it's very like the one Squish found.

"Oh!" I say, without meaning to.

"All right?" asks Mum.

"It's nothing," I say, exiting the website, closing the laptop lid and forcing the fear back down into my stomach.

The sky is super-black tonight but outside my window the countryside is still buzzing with crickets and calls as if it was full sunshine. I sit in the dark, breathing in the cooler air and check my phone. I try texting Florence again, but still there's no answer. So I try ringing her and it just tells me that my call cannot be connected.

Weird.

Perhaps she's run out of battery.

She wouldn't. Would she?

I try ringing again, but no luck.

Perhaps it's the wrong number or something, so I try one more time, checking the number as it dials — not that my phone could actually get it wrong.

Nothing.

I hang out of the window trying to get more cool air and something hits me on the arm.

"Dan!" hisses a voice. "Here!" A tiny torch beam waves from the bottom of the big tree that's next to our garden.

"I thought you were banned from going out?" I say into the darkness.

"I am – so I'm here in secret," comes the whisper. "Come on down."

"Mum's downstairs," I say,

"I know. Come out of the window," says Florence.

"Seriously?" I hang further over the sill and I can see what she means. Below my window, and not very far below, is a small flat roof that must be over the kitchen. From there to the ground is only a short drop. "But how will I get back up?" I hiss.

"I'll give you a leg up. C'mon, I've got a bag of crisps and two lemonades from the fridge – they're all icy and delicious."

It's borderline terrifying but soon I'm sitting on the flat roof and from there I drop to the grass below. It's further than I thought and I clunk my teeth together as I fall. "Oh!"

"Shh," she says, and we both stop, listening for

the sound of Mum realising that I've escaped from my bedroom, but she doesn't, and she even pulls down the kitchen blind and goes back into the living room and turns up the TV.

"Ace," says Florence. "Now, listen. My phone's been confiscated, so I can't ring you, which is why I'm here cos I need to tell you that Mrs Barlow's alive but in a coma at the hospital and that Granddad's quite upset about it; he says too many things are going on at once in a village where nothing's happened for at least forty years and apart from journalists and policemen there's no one on the streets, only locals in the pub, no one wants to eat, and what else was there…?"

Florence pauses and the crickets and a rattle of bottles from somewhere fill the air. I give her a second longer and then butt in.

"Glad she's still alive, s'good." I stop, thinking about the root of that tree and how it had all come out of the ground. "But the tree – I think it was deliberate."

"Really?"

"It was a healthy tree, so why would it just fall down like that?"

"Trees do just fall down," says Florence.

"Not on hot days in the summer, and I think that the hole in the head of the skull has nothing to do with Squish, but everything to do with a gun. In fact, I'm sure of it."

"Oh! Oh!" says Florence. "I wonder if the police have worked that out."

"I'm sure they will have done — but also, when I went to the museum I looked at the records for nineteen seventy-six and found out some stuff about that summer."

"Like?"

"Well, old Mr Fear was buried; he was a local figure, and he had three children. We knew that. Also, the bullion robbery happened almost exactly when old Kenneth Fear died. It's not Thomas at the bottom of the reservoir; he was at the funeral, and he was sent to prison. It's not Sarah — it's a male skull — but the third sibling wasn't at the funeral."

Florence goes quiet for a while. "Derek? Was it Derek in the lake?"

"It can't have been Derek. Laura was married to the person in the lake, her name's Barlow, not Fear — and she's convinced it's her husband in the car.

I can't make it fit together. But back in nineteen seventy-six they *were* looking for a blue Ford."

I can't see Florence's face out here in the dark, but I hear her gasp.

"Blue Ford? So that car was involved in the gold robbery?"

The mozzies buzz around our heads and an owl hoots.

"And now," I say, "years later, a whole bunch of things are all happening at once. A car appears, a body with a hole in the head appears and a woman who is not related to the Fear family is crushed by a tree, not to mention the crows, the bales and the general sense that we shouldn't be poking around in all this. Mrs Barlow told us to be careful."

"But we haven't actually done anything."

"It would be good to know if the body in the river really is from the car in the reservoir," I say, almost to myself.

"I wonder what happened to the gold," she says. "Did you find out if they managed to find it?"

"No, I didn't."

"We need to know," she says.

Something's whining in the air. Mosquitoes.

Hundreds of them. I brush them away from my head.

"Have you thought that the only people who would know where the gold is, if they haven't found it, are the Fear family? Thomas, out of jail by now; Derek—"

"Missing," interrupts Florence.

"And Sarah, wherever she might be."

Chapter 14

It's undignified, but Florence helps me back in through the window and I fall fish-like on to the floor, head first, wedged between the wall and the bed.

"Dan!" Mum's voice. "Dan?"

I hear her feet on the stairs and I try to wriggle myself straight, but I'm still upside down when she comes into my room.

"What on earth are you doing?" she says from the doorway.

"I dropped my charger under the bed," I say,

pulling myself out of the hole.

"Hmmm," says Mum, stomping over and pulling the window shut. "I know it's hot, but keep the mozzies out."

Hours later, lying on top of my bed with the window open, my brain fiddles with all the pieces of the puzzle trying to fit them together. The Fears have to be at the heart of it all. So I sit up and start googling Thomas Fear. I put his name in and all I get is a funeral director in Gloucestershire and a minor cricketer from Yorkshire. Even the bottom of the searches bring nothing useful. I try adding words like "Prison" and "Release" and "Gold Bullion" but they're no good at all.

I lie back down and then almost on the edge of sleep try searching for today's tree accident but it's just "Local woman". Then I try looking up the gold bullion robbery. There are millions of results, and I fall asleep reading through the thousands of theories about what happened to the gold. But I do discover that no one ever found it.

I must have been so tired that I sleep long into the

morning and I'm woken by the sound of Mum's phone ringing downstairs. Standing on the landing, I can hear that she's talking to someone she doesn't know very well; her voice is tense and tight and she's saying the absolute minimum.

"Yes, No. If you have to."

Pulling on a T-shirt I run downstairs into the hall. She's standing by the breeze coming through the front door, the phone close to her ear.

"But I don't think he can tell you anything you don't already know. Anyway, I'm taking him to the museum so you'll have to talk to him later on."

I hear the beep as she closes the call, and fill the kettle noisily from the tap.

"Dan?" Mum comes into the kitchen and slides on to a stool. "Right – I'm totally keeping you with me today. No ifs, no buts. I've had quite enough of those calls from the police. Why can't they write everything down? Surely they don't need to see you twice."

I nod and pour cereal into a bowl, whisk a tea bag out of a cup and slosh milk in both.

"So, another day at the museum? OK?"

Again, I nod my head.

"Good, that's settled." And I can see her breathe with relief.

Outside, the day is less sunny but just as hot. Above us, huge clouds squash in on each other, settling together and bottling the heat beneath them. I think I prefer the blazing sunshine.

Mum grinds the gears until she finds one to get the car moving and we jerk out into the lane and weave our way through the village.

As we leave the houses a bee appears on my side of the windscreen.

"Get it out, Dan, you know I'm allergic," says Mum, opening her window.

I roll mine down and gently remove the bee on a parking ticket.

"Honeybee," I say. "Hope it can find its way home."

We swing round the pub and Mum brakes for a delivery lorry. A second bee appears on the windscreen and I flick it out to join the first.

"Shut the windows and I'll switch on the air conditioning," says Mum as we pick up speed.

She stabs at the buttons and I wince as we bounce

from one verge to the other. Mum probably should never have learned to drive. When I'm older I won't bother – I prefer public transport. It seems safer.

We scrape past an SUV, twanging mirrors with the Mini parked in front of it, and I decide to avoid stress by staring out of the side window.

We're just passing the site of the tree, when I notice two bees clinging to an air vent on my left, and, as I'm staring, another three shoot out into the car.

"Weird," I say, opening my window again.

"Dan – air con – window shut," says Mum, flapping at something in front of her face. I close the windows and turn up the fan for the air conditioning.

The car begins to fill with cooler air, which is blissful, then another bee appears. Where are they coming from? I open the window to shoo it out but the air fills with buzz and what seems like an entire swarm of bees erupts from the air vents.

"Dan! Duck!" shouts Mum, wrenching the wheel to one side.

I close my eyes and mouth and thrash at the door panel. The button has to be there. Ow! My hand rings with the pain of multiple stings as I bash the plastic beside me. Where's the button? Then I'm jerked forward, the seat belt tightens across my chest, and I feel all the little bee bodies bouncing from my face as we hit something solid and I'm winded.

The engine's revving but the bees are revving louder.

I risk opening one eye, and through the huge swarm clinging to the windscreen, I see a wall blocking the road.

I can hear Mum squealing. The roar of the engine stops.

I fumble for the door catch, but the lock must be on and the windows won't open. They don't work without the engine.

Mum's bashing at the side window. "Help!" Her screams are muffled. "Help!"

I thump my window, I get stung, once, twice. "Help!" I shout. And then I do the only thing I can think of. I lean back in my seat, and with my feet kick at the windscreen. The buzzing increases and the bees swarm around my legs, but I kick and kick again, and the windscreen gives way, and like a single huge cloud animal, the bees exit, rushing out through the hole, leaving a few of their clan dead or dying.

"Dan," mumbles Mum. "Dan, call an ambulance."

Mum and I sit on the side of the road. I stare at the car, and stare at my screen, and look at Mum. She's not looking so good. It's been ten minutes since I called the emergency services but I got cut off and I don't know whether to ring again or if the woman on the other end'll call me back. She got the place, and what had happened, and she said they'd come, but she was still talking and she might have had some advice about Mum when the line went dead.

Mum's really pale and her breathing's shallow and panicky, and she's not focusing on me. Her hands are red and swollen, and I'm worried that her lips are beginning to puff up. For the third time I fumble in Mum's bag. I'm sure she has an EpiPen somewhere, but I can't see any sign of it.

"S'all right, Mum, the ambulance is coming," I mutter, gazing up the lane. Why hasn't anyone else passed? Why is there no one around?

Again, I check my screen and as I stare, it bursts

into life. But it's Florence. Not the emergency services woman.

"Dan — I got my phone back—"

I cut her off almost as soon as she starts talking. "Florence — we've had an accident; the car filled up with bees. They can't have got in by themselves. Do you know anyone who keeps bees round here?"

"What?" says Florence. "Bees? What are you on about?"

Behind me an engine roars and I turn round to see an ambulance bowling along the lane towards us. "Forget it!" I say. "Talk to you later."

Even though I'm not really affected by the bee stings, I go in the ambulance to be "kept under observation". The paramedics give Mum a shot of adrenalin and by the time we reach the hospital she's breathing more normally, but she's still swelling up. My hands ache, and then they tingle. Watching my fingers, I can't work out if they're bigger than they were an hour ago. They're definitely different.

The paramedic picks inside Mum's mouth and takes out a little bee body. "I thought so," he says.

"Is it bad?" I ask.

The paramedic doesn't say anything, but I'm pretty sure having a sting inside your mouth isn't good. Mum's the only person I've got. I don't have a dad, or an aunt or an uncle or even a grandma any more and I can't help but watch the worried look on the paramedic's face as she keeps on checking Mum's heart rate.

A little later the paramedic says, "Don't worry," and smiles and checks Mum's mouth again.

We roll along the roads and I peer out of the tiny window, trying not to cry and trying to work out how close to town we are.

"Nearly there. How are you feeling?"

I try to work out how I am feeling. Nervous. Very nervous. And my hands do hurt.

They rush Mum into a bay in the Accident and Emergency department. She's got her eyes open but I'm not sure she's seeing or hearing anything. Everyone kind of ignores me, until a woman in green arrives with a clipboard and starts asking the paramedics questions about Mum and then they point to me.

"Name?" she says.

"Hers? Rachel Kowalski."

"Date of birth?"

I give her all the details and then there's a long time while she fills in all the other squares of her form.

"Next of kin?" she asks.

"What does that mean?"

"In the event of an emergency or something, who should we contact?"

I think about it. It would have been Grandma, but now who? "There's no one, only me," I say pinching my lips together. I will not cry. I really will not.

"Oh, it doesn't matter," she says, smiling for the first time. "Let's see your hands." I show her. On my right hand, my thumb and first finger have become huge red sausages, the skin tight. They throb. So do the two middle fingers on my left hand, and now that I think about it my elbow and knee are pulsing. I look down at my feet. A ring of stings encircle my right leg and the leg of my jeans seems to have become tight.

"How do you feel?" she asks. "Breathless?"

I nod my head. "But that could be because of Mum. Is she going to be OK?"

"I'm sure she'll be fine, but we'll know more in the next hour or so. I'll give you an antihistamine tablet, and see how you are in an hour. You haven't reacted as badly as your mum but if this is the first time you've been stung you probably wouldn't."

She gives me a pill to take and I sit down next to Mum and wait. Machines beep all around, and the person in the bay next to us goes into some kind of crisis and lots of people appear. The curtains are drawn and somebody rushes in with a machine and they all shout, "*Stand back.*"

Mum doesn't move, doesn't acknowledge my hand in hers and I feel worried that I'm the only person watching her. Shouldn't there be a nurse or something? And then I look at the machines and I suppose they're watching her. I keep thinking about the *next of kin* question. Is there someone else I should tell? What would happen if Mum died? There's more beeping and then a woman with a ponytail and a big smile pops her head round the curtain.

"Dan?" she says.

I nod.

"Gotta just do a few checks on your mum. Do

you want to take yourself off to the friends' café? You could get a drink and something to eat. Follow the purple arrows. Come back in forty minutes."

"Like this?" I hold up my oddly shaped hands.

"There are people in pyjamas in there, I wouldn't worry." She smiles again.

I grab Mum's handbag and set off along the corridor towards the café. She's right, it's full of people in pyjamas and volunteers wearing aprons with "Can I help you?" written all over them. Using Mum's bank card I buy myself a doughnut and a chocolate milkshake and sit by the window watching a man cleaning windows on the other side of the courtyard.

A bluebottle buzzes on the outside of the glass and I can't help but flinch.

If I think about it, it's terrifying. The bees. So many of them at once. The black swarm pouring out of the air vents. How? I asked Florence about beekeepers because, deep inside, I'm pretty sure those bees got there on purpose. Does that count as attempted murder?

Someone drops a cup on the other side of the room and I realise that there aren't any tables left, except the one I'm sitting at and I really don't want to talk to anyone, so I leave half a cup of watery hot chocolate and shuffle out of the room.

It's too soon to go back and see Mum. I've got another ten minutes to kill. The corridor is lined with paintings of leaves so I pretend that they're really interesting and wander along, stopping in front of each picture in turn. Behind me trolleys roll past and I lean forward and examine the patterns in a group of brown leaves. I can probably make this last another five minutes.

A toddler races past and trips, and parents rush to rescue it, so I sidestep into a doorway before I realise I've barged into someone's room. Machines beep all around a bed, and I can't see anything of the patient, just bandages and tubes, except for their hair. Strange dirty white crinkly hair. Glancing back to check that no one's watching, I tiptoe across the gap between me and the bed. It *is* her. It's Mrs Barlow. That hair definitely belongs to her. I glance down. At the end of the bed, hanging from the rail, is a clipboard. If I could understand what's written on it, I'd know how she is, could tell Florence. Without picking it up I peer at the writing, which is really poor, and explains almost nothing, just blood pressure and stuff I don't understand, but then I realise that written across the top, in large letters, is a name: Laura Fear.

Fear?

Fear?

Seriously?

Chapter 15

Mum's sitting up and looking a whole lot better when I get back, and the nice woman with the ponytail is chatting to her about archaeology. I'm so relieved I have to blink back the tears.

"Hello, Dan," says the woman. "I think we're going to let you go home, but your mum's going to stay in for a few hours. There's a bus from the hospital back to the village, or do you want a taxi?"

"Perhaps Cat could get you?" Mum reaches across. Her face is all swollen, but I can see a smile trying to pull up the corner of her mouth. "Even if I look like a balloon animal, it sounds like I'll be home for bedtime."

"Don't worry," I say, taking a handful of change from Mum's purse. "I'll get the bus, I've seen it in the village. Bye."

I get up and walk away quickly. I don't want Mum to see the tears that won't stop.

Outside, the air's heavy. It feels as if the clouds have closed down, trapping two weeks' worth of heat two metres off the ground. I wipe my face on my T-shirt. It's hot and itchy. I hadn't noticed but I think I got a sting on my cheek. "Storm's coming," says a woman on the pavement next to me. I nod and check my phone. Loads of messages from Florence queue to be read.

"*Why bees?*"

"*Are you OK?*"

"*Granddad says the car's a write-off.*"

"*Are you in hospital?*"

"*Don't answer that; you are in hospital.*"

"*Coming to the hospital.*"

I look up and can see the bus approaching.

"*Stay put.*"

"I can see you."

Stepping away from the bus stop I stare into all the cars.

My phone buzzes again, and it's Florence.

"Over here — red car," she says, and I look up to see an old Fiat with her granddad at the wheel, arms waving. I'm so relieved, I have to sniff back tears for the second time in ten minutes. Throwing myself into the back seat I slam the door and Florence starts talking immediately.

"So we drove past the car, which is wrapped around a wall, but someone's going to take it away, and I made Granddad stop, so we picked up all the stuff, see, I've got it!" She waves a bag of shoes and Mum's jacket at me. "And then we came on up here, but there were dead bees in there, what happened?"

"Thank you for picking me up," I say to the back of Florence's granddad's head.

"S'all right, lad. We dropped Emma and Adam at the cinema," he says, plummeting down tiny lanes I've never seen before. "Your mum all right?"

"I think she'll be OK, thanks. They'll let her out this evening."

Florence takes a breath, but doesn't say anything, then obviously decides she can. "So how did the bees get in the car? Did you drive through a swarm?"

"They came through the air con," I say. "Masses of them – it took a few seconds."

Florence goes quiet and stares out of the windscreen. Then she looks back at me.

"Exactly," I say. "That's why I asked if anyone kept bees."

"Lots of people, I think," she says.

"There are bees at Colside and Thrawthwaite," says her granddad. "Also Old Mrs Tapstowe used to keep them, and some farms have 'em. Dunno which. Keeping bees is more popular than it was. But it would have to be someone that picked up a swarm in a box – you couldn't take them out of a hive at this time of year. They wouldn't come." He swings the car past a waiting white van and we pop up in the village, two hundred metres from the pub. "How are your hands, lad? Do you fancy some chips?"

Florence and I sit in the beer garden, although the clouds are now so low and heavy they must be about to burst and the air feels thick with the promise of rain. I look around to make sure that nobody is listening. "I saw Mrs Barlow at the hospital."

Florence, caught mid-chip, turns and holds her hand up over her mouth. A curious little noise comes out of her mouth, which I imagine is an enquiry. "Wha'?"

"She's in a room off a corridor and I stepped in there to avoid a trolley – anyway, that's not the point. The point is, that she is in there and she's all hooked up to wires and pipes, and, wait for it, her surname is Fear."

Florence nearly chokes this time. "Fear? How?"

"Suppose she was married to a Fear. One of the three children. Derek."

Florence swirls her finger around in her drink, making the ice cubes bounce against the side of the glass.

"Could be. So there's Thomas – he's the one who was involved in the robbery and went to prison. Derek's the one who's been at the bottom of the lake. Then there's Sarah. What happened to her?"

"She'd be more than sixty by now."

A family come out and sit at the table next to

us, the children demanding crisps and the parents looking exhausted.

"And someone has to be behind the birds, the tree, the bales and the bees," I say.

"Which put your mum in hospital," says Florence. "And Laura Fear/Barlow in hospital."

"Now, you two," says Florence's granddad, coming out of the pub and loading up a tray with empty glasses. He puts it on the table we're sitting at and leans forward so that we can hear him, but no one else can. "I want you to stay here until Dan's mum is out of hospital." He glances over his shoulder to check for earwiggers. "I want to be able to find you at all times. What with everything that's going on around here, I can't risk you running around." He places two more glasses on the tray and stands back. "Apart from anything else the place is swarming with journalists and I don't want you talking to any of them. Understand?" He's smiling, but he sounds deadly serious. There's real warning in the tone of his voice.

"OK," I say.

"Yes, OK, Granddad," says Florence, nodding like crazy, so much so that I'm pretty sure she has no intention of staying put for long.

I follow her round the back of the bar and we slip through a door marked *Private*. Steep stairs ascend to a cosy collection of bedrooms and Florence leads the way to her tiny room that sits over the garden, the bed under the window and barely enough room to put our feet on the floor. The wallpaper is of cars and planes and is all bumpy.

"Sorry about the room," she says. "It was my uncle's and I think Granddad's before that. No one's decorated it since the beginning of time. Emma's got the bigger room on the other side."

"I like it; it's got character," I say. "And it's brilliant being able to see everyone come and go below."

We can. We can see both sides of the wall, the garden and the approach to the front of the pub. Three men and a woman sit at a bench on the tarmac by the main door. They're huddled together, smoking cigarettes and frantically typing things into their phones. Florence points at them. "Journalists," she says.

In a car on the other side of the road is a man,

possibly asleep or possibly talking to someone on a phone. "He's one too," she says. "He's been out there since yesterday."

"I wonder if they know if the body in the reservoir is the same one we found?" I say, looking down at the journalists huddling by the front of the pub.

"We could ask," says Florence, peering down at them. "The man on the right looks OK. I mean, he doesn't look like he's going to eat us or anything. Let me just..." She pulls her braids round into two massive bunches and turns to face me. "Younger?" she asks.

"Totally," I say. And she does; she looks about eight. It's remarkable.

"And this?" she says, swapping her black sweatshirt that makes her look like a cat burglar for a pink one with a silver heart sewn on the front.

"Yup." I nod. "Perfect."

Chapter 16

A minute later and we're tiptoeing past the bar window. Strictly speaking we're still kind of in the pub, or at least we could reach it in less than a second.

Florence wanders over to the journalists and pulls that innocent big-eyed puppy look. "S'cuse me, do you know anything about the bones in the river?"

The man looks up from his phone. He looks as if he hasn't slept, hasn't washed and has lived on coffee for the last month. His eyes are red and his skin's unnaturally pale. I can see from the way his eyes narrow that he hasn't entirely bought the innocent puppy look.

"Why? Do you know anything?"

He looks from Florence to me and I can imagine that he's working out the connection between two children that found the bones and the two children standing in front of him. Although the children that found the bones were nearly teenagers. This girl is about nine, and the boy has a horrible disease that leaves lumps all over his face. I smile. I know my smile is wonky. I must look deranged.

"No," says Florence. "We don't but we want to go swimming and we want to know if it's safe in the river and no one will tell us."

Now the other journalists have noticed us and their focus moves away from their mobile phones.

"It's fine," I say. "We'll just go to the swimming pool in town."

"Hey, what happened to your hand, kid?" says the woman. "That looks nasty."

I look down at my giant sausage fingers and just as I say, "Bees," Florence says, "It's genetic."

"Oh?" says the first journalist, and Florence skips out round the side of the table and pats her hair, saying, "C'mon, let's go."

I sweep past the little group and together the two of us walk just short of a run along the street and towards the church. We don't say anything and swing in through the gate that leads to the churchyard.

"Phew," says Florence, leaning against the wall. "Do you think they followed us?"

Clambering on top of one of the ancient graves I look under the yew trees towards the front of the pub. The journalists are still there. Two on their phones, the other three smoking and texting. "We're OK," I say. Wobbling on my perch, I survey the cemetery. From here the grave of Kenneth Fear does look completely different from the others. It's almost convex when the others are concave. Jumping down, I wander over to take a look. As I cross the shorn brown grass, a single drop falls from the sky and splats on to the back of my hand.

It's just one. And no more fall for another five minutes.

The grass on the grave is thinner and more

burned than the surrounding area. I rub my hand over the surface and think something almost too ridiculous to share. "It's hot," I say. "Hotter than the grass over there."

Florence stands behind me, her palms open flat, gazing up at the sky. "I swear I got rained on," she says, dabbing at her sweatshirt. "Yeah, look, that's definitely a raindrop. Oooh, that's good, we'll have a proper cloudburst if we're lucky."

"Florence?" I say. "Could you just tell me if I'm crazy – is the ground hotter here, or here?"

Raising her eyebrows, she crouches down and rubs her hand across the ground, over the grave and over the grass alongside. "Stones," she pronounces finally. "The ground is full of stones. Big stones. They get hot and retain the heat," she says, sounding like a science book.

"Really?" I say. "That hot?"

Sitting back on my heels I study the ground. It's scuffed where we dug away the earth from the headstone the other day, but it looks as if someone's tried to strip the turf back since. Or perhaps it was always like that?

"Hey, what was that?" Florence stands and

stares towards the far side of the cemetery. The corner where the old compost heaps and yew trees compete for space. Where there are no bodies, or headstones. "I'd swear I saw something move."

"A cat?" I say, standing.

"No – too big and too high."

We both stare into the mess of branches and briars that inhabit the far corner of the graveyard. They're behind the giant yew trees. It's dark over there. Private. I don't think either of us wants to walk towards the dark corner until single drops of rain multiply, catching up with each other and bouncing off the leaves, vanishing instantly into the warm stones. The pattering intensifies and instinctively I step forward into the crunchy skeletons of twig and fern that lie thick on the ground below the trees.

"I didn't see anything," I say, peering into the thicket that stretches beyond.

Beside me Florence nods. Behind us the rain has turned from individual drops to a steady hiss, and a smell like freshly baked biscuits fills the air. "I definitely saw something, or someone," she says in the smallest of voices.

The rain increases and becomes so loud on the leaves and the detritus below the trees that I can't hear my feet crunching. I can't hear anything. I stretch my hand out into the deluge and let the raindrops cool my bee stings.

"We're behind Mrs Barlow's house," says Florence, pointing to the wall beyond the trees. "Do you think someone went in through that door?"

"There's only one person I can think of who'd do that."

Florence's eyes widen. "Thomas Fear." She looks around the churchyard. "Let's get out of here."

With the rain falling hard on my head, trickling deliciously down my back and instantly plastering my jeans to my legs, I skim over the churchyard, getting its darkness and secrets behind me until we both clang back out into the lane. Gutters block with leaves and within seconds gush on to the road and into gardens. It's as if the landscape's been waiting and now it's filled with action and colour. Running with our hands over our heads we charge back towards the pub and splatter past the journalists now smoking under an umbrella, through the door, along the passage and up the stairs.

"Soaked," says Florence, throwing herself on the bed.

"Completely," I say, shaking my head so that the raindrops spray the room.

"Dan!" she laughs, and yanks off her pink sweatshirt, replacing it with the black one. For a few minutes we sit in the window watching the rain sweep the dust of weeks along the side of the lane and down the drain. Water pours from the porch roof and fills empty pint glasses left out on tables. A couple, who have pinned themselves against the hedge in the garden, give up and rush into the pub, clutching their glasses in their hands.

Cars splash along the road and it all smells incredible.

Kneeling alongside each other, watching it all unfold, I say, "It must be Thomas Fear. He must be living in Mrs Barlow's house."

"The Fear house," says Florence.

"The house he grew up in. Perhaps he still owns it."

"And Laura Barlow's been living there all these years waiting for her husband Derek to come back."

"Thomas would want to stop us investigating."

"And he'd want to stop Laura talking about what

happened in the past."

"Enough to push a tree on her? Why not just kill her in her house. He's right there."

"Yeah, I admit that bit sounds weird, but who else could it be?"

We stare out of the window, thinking. Little scraps of dried moss skid down the roof and catch in the gutter below us. I lean forward to release them and let the water through.

"Why would he come back? Why would he risk being recognised? She wouldn't be the only one who knew who he was. That's insane."

"He must have a really good reason to come back," says Florence.

"A really good reason to nearly kill my mother," I say, swallowing sudden tears. "I mean, she could have died. Who would do that? Put bees in a car?"

"I think he was trying to kill you."

We sit in silence watching the rain. I yank my mind back from Mum, from the bees and try to think about reasons and Thomas Fear and why he's here.

"There's always the gold," I say. "That would be a really good reason."

Chapter 17

The deluge hammers down all afternoon and we stay watching the gate of the churchyard from the shelter of Florence's bedroom as evening comes on. It's hard to keep it in sight, but we can see the gate and we can just about see Laura's house.

As it gets darker, we watch for lights coming on, but the house stays dim and gloomy.

"Do you think he'll even come out?" says Florence.

"I reckon we'll see him after dark," I reply.

"Look at this rain!" she says, holding the palm

of her hand up to catch it. "It's the kind of rain I really love. Thick, heavy drops, oh wow! The BEST! Look at the way it's making rivers in the road."

Yellow street-light reflections cover the lane and the car of the sleeping journalist changes from red to dull grey. Although it's only eight o'clock it feels like night is properly setting in and the downpour gets more intense. We keep the light off in Florence's bedroom so that we can see the street without being seen ourselves.

"Do you think he's been looking at the grave too?" I say, finally voicing the thing that's been going through my head, but is too ludicrous to be true.

"How d'you mean?"

"Some of the grass has gone from the top of the grave. I think someone's been looking for something."

"What?"

"The gold," I say.

"Seriously?" Florence goes quiet for ages. "There," she says eventually. "Look!"

Staring until my eyeballs hurt, I concentrate on the darkness around the church gate.

"There, just beyond – see?"

I do see. She's right. On the far side of the gate, deep in the shadows of the trees is a darker shape. It moves and then stops. Moves again, and almost invisibly slips through the gate into the churchyard, vanishing immediately in the shadows of the gravestones. It looks like a man. A tall man. Carrying something. A spade perhaps?

"I saw that," I say. "Definitely someone."

"Someone who didn't want to be seen," she says.

Now we've seen him I think we're both wondering what to do. But we're stopped from doing anything at all by the arrival of a Land Rover and Mum steps out into the rain, looking almost normal under the street lights.

Downstairs, the pub is full of chattering strangers filing news reports from their laptops. I see the journalist we talked to and stay back in the corridor as Mum is ushered through by Florence's granddad. One of the journalists looks as if he's about to ask them questions but he doesn't, and Mum stumbles into the tiny back room where we're waiting.

The moment Mum sees me, she grabs me and

holds me tight. We stand together in the middle of the room while Florence bobs around taking things off chairs and Cat pauses awkwardly in the doorway before turning and plunging back out into the rain.

"Dan," says Mum. "Dan."

Mum holds me away from her and looks at me. I gaze back at her. She looks like she's been in a boxing ring fighting a kangaroo. Her eye and lips are still horribly big, and when she smiles her face kind of cracks rather than stretches, but she's still Mum. She smooths hair from my forehead and then examines my hands, which are red but slightly less enormous and just beginning to itch. Mum sinks on to a chair, and Florence's granddad brings in a pint of lime juice and soda. The little room is quiet and smells of woodsmoke and a little of Squish, who rests his head on Mum's knee and looks at her as if he's never seen anyone so weird.

"Hello, dog," she says, letting her hand fall on his neck. "And thank you, Florence's grandfather."

"Trevor," he says, sitting on the arm of the sofa. "Now, I'm honestly minded to think, what with everything, that you should pack up and go home. There's too much trouble here, and you –" he looks at me – "seem to be caught in the middle of it."

"Did they identify the bones?" asks Florence. "Has anybody said?"

"None of your business, missy," says her grandfather.

"But have they?" Florence asks again. "I just want to know if we were right about the car."

"You were," says her granddad. "They reckon they're from the lake. Same flora or something. Been there forever. But no one's got any idea how they got moved to the river." He looks at Squish. "It's only cos of him you found them."

"Yes!" cries Florence, punching the air.

"Don't know why you're so delighted," says Trevor. "That was someone's body."

"Yes but it means we were right," says Florence. "There was a body in the car. It's just that someone moved it before the police turned up."

Cat comes in from the car park through the back door, wiping her wellies on the way. "How are we doing?" she asks.

I glance over at Mum and see that her eyes are

almost closed. She must be exhausted, and I want to be on my own with her. "Can we go now? I'm tired."

Florence's granddad looks at both of us and snorts, before standing up and going back out into the corridor. "Well, like I say, I think you should consider skedaddling. Those bees — well, it was odd. I've never heard of such a thing. And the tree, and the car. You're in the middle of it, and I'd hate for you to get hurt." He looks at Florence and points at her, and then back to me. "Either of you. There are things going on in this village that I don't understand."

A bell rings at the front, and he steps away, his boots clunking on the lino back to the bar.

There's a moment's silence and then Cat claps her hands together and says, "Well, whatever Trevor says, I think I should take you back to your cottage now. Ready?"

I nod. Mum stands and we follow Cat out into the rain, bundling into the Land Rover, three in a row on the front seat. As we leave, Florence sticks a piece of paper into my hand and waves goodbye.

The Land Rover trundles through the lanes of

the village. It's not really far enough to need a lift, but I can sense that Mum doesn't want to walk, and anyway the rain's hard enough to mean that small rivers are now running down the streets even though the air's still hot. Florence was right, all this rain does feel like a monsoon.

Cat pulls to a halt outside the cottage and Mum gives me the key while Cat hands me an umbrella. I struggle with the door and we bundle in, laughing and wet, jamming in the entrance.

"What a day," says Mum, shaking the umbrella and leaning it against the front door. "I'm starving, and I don't want anyone to see me eating!"

She heads off into the kitchen while I take off my trainers. Ten hours ago, those trainers saved our lives.

"Just a cup of tea would be good," says Cat, following Mum inside.

"Dan," says Mum from the kitchen. "Dan – have you been back to the house today?"

"No," I say, wandering into the kitchen. "No, why?"

Mum's staring at the pepper and salt pots.

"They weren't there this morning. I put them in

the cupboard."

"You sure?" says Cat, staring at the immaculate white countertop scattered with brown coffee rings.

I come and stand beside them. "I don't remember."

"Well, I do, and look at the toaster. It's been plugged in on the other side."

I look at both sides of the kitchen. She's right. It has.

"Mum," I say. "I think you're right."

Chapter 18

Mum rings the police.

"Don't," I say. "They won't believe us."

But she does, and although Cat looks ready to fall asleep on the sofa, she stays and it's almost midnight before they turn up. It's the tired man in uniform who has been twice before and he looks at the kitchen surfaces with an expression of disinterest.

"So someone came in, and moved your salt and pepper pots?"

"And the toaster," says Mum.

"And it wasn't you, young man?" he says, giving me a hard stare.

"No," I say. "Mum and I were in hospital because we got attacked by bees that were put in our car."

"Shhh, Dan," says Mum. "I think that was just unlucky."

"Bees?" says the policeman. "Bees?"

"A swarm of bees were in our car. They made their way through the air-conditioning unit and into the car. Mum got badly stung, and, look — look at my hand."

There's a long silence while the policeman peers at Mum's face and then with his huge fingers writes things in his notebook. "So how come you didn't report it?"

"Because they were in hospital?" says Cat from the end of the sofa.

"Do you want to report it?" he asks, ignoring Cat. "You could. I mean, it's unusual. I've never heard of it happening naturally."

"It happens in other countries," says Cat.

"I don't know what the point of reporting it is," says Mum.

"But—" I begin, but the policeman's already on

his feet and heading towards the door.

"Aren't you going to take a look in the kitchen?" says Mum.

"No," says the policeman. "If there's no sign of a break-in and no damage done, and nothing missing, I honestly can't do much. So goodnight, all." And he strides towards the door, opens it and steps out into the pouring rain.

"Well," says Mum. "That was hardly worth it."

"No," says Cat. "I thought at least he'd ask if we'd seen anyone hanging about."

I remember the shadow in the churchyard and let out a tiny squeak.

"What is it?" says Mum.

"Nothing – it's just we did see someone in the village."

"Really," says Cat, looking the most animated I've seen her all evening.

"It might be nothing. We didn't exactly see anyone, just a shadow," I backtrack. "Not sure what they looked like."

"Weird to be sloping around the village in the tipping rain," says Mum.

"Could have been a journalist or someone," says Cat.

"They weren't a journalist. They were carrying a spade."

"Really?" Cat looks up at the ceiling as if she's thinking. "There are a few itinerants around here. People who live up in the woods. We're always on the lookout. But I haven't heard anything recently. You couldn't actually describe anyone, though?"

"No – not really. Not sure what age, height, any of that." Suddenly I'm exhausted. "Anyway, I'm going to bed."

Mum gives me a hug and I wander up the stairs. Mum says goodnight to Cat and I hear the Land Rover start up and rumble away. Keeping the lights off, I open the window. The rainfall is still massive, continuous streams of water sheeting down over the road. Pulling Florence's note from my pocket I read it again. *Meet you at the churchyard. Text me when you can get there.*

Sitting on my bed, fully dressed, I rummage in my bag for my waterproof. It's not really very waterproof, but it'll help. My jeans are already damp, so that doesn't matter. I listen for Mum thumping on the stairs. The bathroom noises. Teeth brushing. The toilet flushing. And then I wait for the click of her bedroom door.

I wait a little longer and open my door. There's still a light under Mum's door so I sit on my bed waiting for it to go out. Then, a few minutes later, I hear the soft sound of Mum's night breathing. It's not quite snoring, but nearly. The house hums with the rain, so I reckon there's no way she'll hear me tiptoe down the stairs, and I'm guessing she won't be able to hear the front door.

Before stepping out into the downpour, I text Florence and then, armed with Cat's umbrella, I slip out on to the street. Immediately everything is about water. Water pouring in rivulets down the tarmac, streaming over the sides of the umbrella, accumulating in huge dark puddles that reflect the street lights and catch me out straight away so that within a minute I'm soaking.

No one's around, and most of the houses are dark. It feels as if I'm invisible myself and I hang close to the walls, trying to keep myself hidden. Down a couple of alleys and I reach the pub, which is also dark, but Florence's waiting in the porch, practically invisible. She darts across to join me under the umbrella and, saying nothing, we slosh along the lane to the church.

The church has a single light on the clock. Otherwise it's all in shadow. The churchyard itself is black fading to blacker.

"Is this a good idea?" she whispers.

"No," I say. "But we're here now. C'mon."

Stopping by the gate, between us we click open the latch and push it open, but it resists us and then, when it moves it lets out a long mournful groan. I freeze and Florence scuttles past me to hide just inside the wall. I follow, still holding the umbrella, and get hooked up on the metal arch that goes over the gateway.

"Shhh." Florence giggles from the shadows, and I crouch down beside her.

We've made no plan, but I think we both know that we're looking at the grave. We're looking to see what the shadow has been up to.

My legs are already soaked, and I can feel the damp creeping up my jeans to my bum but it won't take long. We'll be back in our beds really soon. Slowly we creep across the churchyard and stop at the main doors. I can't see Florence's face, but she takes my arm and together we creep round the end of the building, and stop.

There, exactly where I'd expect, is a yellow beam of light. It's a torch lying on the ground and it's shining at a pair of boots. The boots seem to be staying still but there's a spade moving over the surface, lumps of brown turf collecting at the side and something in the hole that the digger is finding very heavy.

"Gold?" Florence murmurs.

As we watch the rain gets even heavier and there's a distant rumble of thunder.

We shuffle closer together, sheltering under the umbrella, pressed against the side of the church. The thunder rumbles again and then lightning flickers through the clouds. I don't like thunderstorms; I've never liked them and I especially don't like them when I'm out in the open.

I'm just thinking of running for the gate when there's an enormous flash in which the churchyard is lit up like daylight and I get to see a tall man, digging. Just as suddenly it goes dark and it's followed by a massive crash and the air shudders and both of us scream. The lightning comes again and the man looks over to us, and this time I see his face, dark eyes, his mouth in an O, shouting something. Florence leaps up and runs for the gate, and I'm right with her, all thoughts of the umbrella abandoned, but even through the pelting rain I can hear his footsteps on the path behind us.

"Run!" shouts Florence.

"I am!" I yell, and head across the graveyard, leaping over and round the stones, but the feet are closing in on my left and I'm not going to make it to the gate so I veer off to the side, stumbling in the dark and nearly falling headlong as I run into the older part of the cemetery. Dodging the gaping graves and tumbled monuments I race for the wall. The feet behind me are struggling too, both of us only finding our way round the gaping graves when lightning illuminates the whole scene. Plunged back into the dark, I head for where I thought I saw a line of trees hanging over the wall. Rocks and roots snare my feet, but soon I can feel that there must be something above me changing the feel of the rain from steady to drippy. Reaching up I grab at air until I find a branch and using every ounce of strength in my fingertips I walk my feet up the trunk until I can hook my knee over the branch. Fear takes me further and before the next lightning strike I'm sitting in the tree, surrounded by leaves, watching the man searching the gravestones and hoping that lightning chooses the church tower rather than my tree as the shortest way to earth. Beyond the stooping figure, nearer the church, Florence melts into the dark of one of the buttresses. Although the rain's beating down around my head, I daren't move or I'll slip, and he'll hear; he's bound to hear.

The thunder rumbles above me and the rain becomes bucket heavy and still I can sense the digger man crashing around. During the next rumble of thunder, I pull myself upright so that I'm standing on the branch and look over the back of the wall. All I can see is black. If I jumped, I'd be abandoning Florence, but perhaps he thinks we both made it over the wall anyway.

I don't know what to do. It's too risky to jump. There might be anything or nothing on the other side of the wall. I'm going to have to wait it out.

Chapter 19

It must be an hour. Surely. The rain hasn't stopped at all, I'm desperate to move and then I see the headlights of a distant milk float trundle along the road and stop.

Through the leaves I check for the digging man, but I can't see him and the way through to the gate seems clear. I creak my legs straight and risk dropping back into the churchyard. Straightening my legs is agony and the ground hurts when I land, the soles of my feet tingling with pins and needles. Like some ancient bent-over old man, I hobble across the uneven ground, heading for the place where I last saw Florence.

She's gone.

Stopping for a minute to let the blood pump through my legs, I lean against the wall of the church, out of reach of the gargoyles spouting water into the huge drain that surrounds the building. When the pins and needles subside, I angle my wet trainers, letting a small river run from the inside through the gauzy patches on the instep. If I went swimming in my clothes I couldn't be any wetter. I want to go home and change, but I can't leave without knowing what happened to Florence. My hands shaking, I reach into my pocket and touch the button on the side of my phone. Can I pull it out without the screen showing?

I'm going to risk it.

"*Where are you?*" I text, and then I jam the phone back in my soggy pocket.

Staying close to the building, I creep along the wall and swing round the end of the buttress so that I can see the gateway. The gate's closed and there's still no sign of Florence.

Or the digger man.

The milk float's right outside the gate now. The milk person's clattering bottles. It sounds really normal and I calm my breathing, thinking happy thoughts of milkshakes and bowls of cereal.

Must keep my mind calm. Waves. Clouds. Rivers. I step out from behind the church and walk round the front of the building until I'm standing outside the main doors. There's nobody else here. I turn 360 degrees and check that I'm right. No, there really isn't anyone else here. Suddenly, without the fear and adrenalin that's been keeping me going, I can feel the water dripping down the back of my jeans, the ache in my legs. The cold and the extraordinary tiredness.

Ignoring it, I turn on my phone torch and pick my way over the soggy ground towards where the man was digging. I don't honestly like the idea of peering into a grave, I might find another pile of bones.

Instead it's a mound of messy turf and muddy earth jammed back together in a hurry, but flatter than I remember it. Scraping the clods to one side, I peer underneath. There are small rectangular imprints on the earth, not neat but all haphazard, as if someone had a load of little bricks, threw them into a grave and then covered them, years later deciding to dig them up.

That figures.

I'm standing, staring, thinking, with the rain hammering on my head, dripping from my nose, when Florence appears beside me.

"Oh! You made me jump!" I say.

"Sorry," she says. "Where were you?"

"Up a tree – how about you?"

"I climbed inside the compost heap. I was visited by hedgehogs and I'm totally frozen."

"Did you see him go?"

She shakes her head and points at the squares in the mud. "What do you reckon?"

"If you'll keep watch, I'll see if there's anything else underneath."

"Go on then," she says.

I've only got my fingernails so I claw at the ground and in three handfuls I reach a layer of sacking.

I glance round at Florence.

"Go on," she says again.

The crust of earth on top of the sacking pings away as I pull it and I get the faintest glint of something through the fibres. I was right.

"Is that what I think it is?" says Florence over my shoulder.

Scraping the earth from the top, I poke my finger through the largest hole and pull the sacking apart. We both lean down to look.

Neither of us say anything and then she says, "Cover it up, Dan. Cover it up and let's get out of here. We need to leave as fast as we can."

As we run from the churchyard, we pass the milk float, which is standing in the water collecting on the main road. We stop outside the pub, our backs flat to the wall.

"I'm going to go home before I freeze to death. I'll get Mum to call the police."

Florence nods.

"You OK?" I say.

"Just thinking. Do we have to tell anyone? We could dig it up and keep it ourselves. Or at least some of it. Couldn't we?" She looks at me, the water streaming down her face, and smiles.

"Seriously?" I say. "With that guy wandering around? Who probably saw us in the lightning?

And old Laura in hospital and an ancient skull with a hole through it?"

"You're quite right," she laughs. "We must tell someone, now, straight away. I'm so cold, Dan. But gold, Dan – we just found a load of gold."

"Gold. I know." I stare at the water circling and vanishing down the drain in the road. "Isn't it terrifying?"

Chapter 20

It turns out that running in sodden trainers and soaked jeans is practically impossible. The road is now a river and if anything, the rain's harder. I get to our door and fumble with the key, my hands too cold to function. It's the middle of the night, so I peel off my jeans and trainers while I'm still outside, and chuck the rest of my clothes on top of them. The house is silent, so I creep upstairs and shut myself straight in the bathroom. The water comes out cold, but I'm so cold it feels hot and I have to slowly bring up the heat so that I can bear it.

After ten minutes in the steaming bathroom, I step out and wrap myself in a towel before tiptoeing back into the bedroom.

My feet are still white with cold, so I put on two pairs of socks and practically all my other clothes until I can barely move, then I pad downstairs, stuff my wet clothes in the washing machine and put the kettle on. I'm so tired. My phone battery is totally flat and I put it on charge. In a few minutes I could ring the police. Or I could wait and get Mum to do it, but I'm not quite sure how to explain about the gold. How would I have found it? How would I not have found it earlier this evening? Could I have known about it and then decided not to tell anyone until now?

The more I think about it the worse the story sounds.

My legs sag, and I go back to my bed with my phone. Shall I call the police? What do I say? I lie back on my bed and pull the duvet over. For the first time in ages I'm not too hot in the bed.

Which is why I fall into a deep unbroken sleep.

I wake to gentle knocking at the door. A voice calls

through the letter box. "Hello?" Female, but not Florence. Cat?

Oh no – it's morning!

"Hello!"

It *is* Cat. I can't ignore her. Feeling like I'm coming up from the bottom of a well I stumble down the stairs.

"Hi there, Dan," she says as I open the door. "I was worried about your mum after last night. How is she?"

"Er, come in," I say. "She's still in bed, but..."

At the top of the stairs Mum's door opens. "Cat? Is that you? Make Cat a cuppa, Dan. Isn't this rain lovely? I'll be down in a mo."

Cat and I stand in the kitchen. It's awkward and I can't help looking towards the bottom of the stairs every few seconds hoping to see Mum, but all I can hear are the shower pipes gurgling.

"You look exhausted, Dan," says Cat. "What have you been up to?"

So I tell her. It sounds even crazier than I expect it to and part of me wonders if it was all a weird dream.

"Um – well, after you left last night, I – um,

couldn't get back to sleep. I think it was the rain – so, I went out again."

"What, in the middle of the night?"

"Early morning," I lie and feel my ears heat up. "And I kind of wandered around, towards the churchyard."

"Oh yes?"

"And there was a man there – although he'd gone by the time I got there."

Cat screws up her face as if she's trying to understand what I mean.

"Anyway – early this morning – we, I mean, I – looked around the churchyard and someone had been digging in one of the graves."

"A gravedigger?"

"Not a new grave – an old one belonging to a bloke named Kenneth Fear."

Cat raises her eyebrows. "Really?"

"And there were these blocks, under the soil, like, um, ingots?" I realise it sounds totally ludicrous. My voice shrinks. "So I want to ring the police."

Cat looks sideways at me. "I don't know. I mean, gold in the churchyard?"

"I know – it sounds really weird, but I'm sure it's

gold. It was metal. Yellow metal."

"Tell you what," says Cat with a long sigh. "I'll go and take a look. I've got full waterproofs in the car. You stay here, out of trouble – OK? And if I find anything – I'll call the police."

"OK," I say, massively relieved. The idea that an adult is actually taking charge almost makes me cry.

She stomps out into the rain and guns the Land Rover off down the road.

Mum arrives in the kitchen. "Where did Cat go?" I open my mouth to tell her but she's not listening. "Did she have to milk the cows or something? Ah well, never mind." She starts to make some toast. "Now, Dan. No digging today, far too wet. If it keeps raining like this, the site may be back underwater by this evening. I'm going to make a few phone calls, then why don't we settle down with a movie?"

Chapter 21

Half an hour later, Cat rings Mum.

Mum sits on the end of the sofa listening. "He did what?" She gives me a look that chills my blood. "No, I understand. Thank you so much, Cat – I'm so sorry you've been put to so much trouble. Dan's always had a bit of an overactive imagination!" She glares at me again.

"Did she find anything?" I whisper.

I can hear Cat at the other end of the phone. "...lots going on. And the films they watch these days."

"OK, I'll tell him," says Mum. "Before grounding him for a month, yes!"

She switches off the call and faces me. "What on earth were you thinking, Dan! Creeping about in a graveyard at night and forcing Cat to investigate some old nonsense! What must she think of us!"

"But what did she find?"

Mum sighs. "Absolutely nothing."

I frown. "But that doesn't..."

Mum gives me a quick hug and throws herself down on the end of the sofa. "Dream on, sunshine – there ain't no gold in them there hills. C'mon, let's go on with the movie."

I sit next to Mum, staring at the carpet. Nothing? Really? So what was the guy doing in the churchyard?

For a moment I'm stunned and then something begins to dawn. Something I've been ignoring. That's been bothering me. Distant noises come from the TV and I'm aware of the storm beating on the windows.

"Mum, can you get DNA from a body that's been at the bottom of a lake?"

"Yes. Well, probably."

"And does anyone that's done one of those family DNA test things – can the police access their DNA? I mean, has it happened? Could they find DNA on an ancient body and then find a living relative?"

Mum nods. "A fair bit in the States and a little bit over here – why?"

"Just wondering."

Mum's phone buzzes. While she's talking, I run upstairs to get mine.

Good, it's mostly charged and there are only three messages from Florence.

"Where are the police?"

"Did you even call them?"

"Shall I do it?"

I message back.

"Told Mum's friend, Cat. She went to check. Says there was nothing there. But. . ."

"But what?" Florence messages back before I've even put the phone down. *"Makes no sense."*

"You're right." Putting on shorts, trainers and a T-shirt, I message her: *"Coming over."*

"Going out to watch the rain," I say to Mum. She nods; she's still on her phone. I steal Mum's waterproof and leg it out of the door before she notices.

The rain patters on the hood and splashes on to my feet, but the good thing about bare legs is that they don't mind getting wet. For a second I play with the water, damming it and letting it pool before nudging aside the barrier and watching the resulting wave sweep small islands of debris off down the lane.

I paddle off through the village. In places the water is as deep as my ankles and some of the houses have sandbags against their doors like they know something.

A moment later Mum texts.

"Cat rang. She needs a hand with something. Won't be long. X."

I nearly turn back.

The pub's lights are on and it looks cosy, especially as the journalists seem to have found somewhere else to hang out. My phone pings and I bend over to read it, keeping most of the water off the screen.

"Can see you. Will be out in a sec."

There's a flash of white at the window of

Florence's bedroom and then she appears at the front door. She's carrying an umbrella, dressed in an enormous coat and wellingtons and doesn't look a bit like Florence.

"'Lo," she says, shuffling over the road. "Shall we take a look?"

I nod and, with the rain pouring from the bottom of Mum's coat all over my feet, we scuttle to the churchyard. There's nobody there, and we run for the shelter of the porch.

"We can go and look in the grave again, just to be sure," I say.

Florence nods and with the growing sensation that Mum's waterproof is not waterproof we shuffle to Kenneth Fear's grave.

"Oh!" I say.

"Oh, indeed," says Florence.

The scratchy layer of turf is totally stripped back now, and fresh red earth shows beneath. What's noticeable is that the whole thing seems to have sunk.

"Something doesn't add up," I say.

We stand under the cascading umbrella like characters from *Totoro* both staring into the grave.

"Try the house?" I say, pointing towards Mrs Barlow's cottage.

Florence shrugs. "Guess so," she says. "Front door?"

"What do we do if he answers it?" I say.

"I'll think of something," she says, which doesn't reassure me at all.

We turn from the grave and drip through the cemetery towards the gate. Without a word we turn left and walk round the chaotic hedge that surrounds Laura Barlow's garden. The storm drains are blocked and a stream has formed down the side of the road, swooshing twigs and leaves in its wake, racing off along the main street. The gate is silent, and all too quickly we find ourselves standing on the paving outside the front door.

Florence knocks and we wait under the dripping porch for someone to answer.

Nothing happens, so she knocks again.

I stand back to look up at the windows. It's all dark in there. While Florence stands on the doorstep I shuffle along the front of the cottage, brushing against tall bushes that cascade water down my shins. I reach the front room. The curtains are half closed, but not totally, and there's a light on. Pressing my nose against the glass, I peer into the gloom. It's quite difficult to see. The room's dismal, with a picture of a pink ballerina hanging at an angle over a tiled fireplace. The wallpaper is grubby primrose, and there's a sofa with a stretchy lavender cover placed next to a battered leather armchair.

There's also something on the floor. Something dark and lumpy. Pressing myself closer to the glass I try to make out what it is. It could be a coat or a rug?

"Dan – Dan," hisses Florence. "The door's open."

"Is it?" I call back. I try tilting my head so that I can see through the cleanest part of the glass, but I still can't make it out. Not properly. Although...

"Shall I go in?" she calls.

"Um, what?" I answer. "Go in? Hang on."

Brushing past the floppy plants I set off another cascade of water and reach the front door just as Florence decides to go through it. "Hello! Hello!" she calls. "Anyone home?"

I follow, but I'm scared. I want to find Thomas Fear, but I'd imagined it would be out in the open, not in a house. A weird scary house at that. It smells of damp, or mice, or both, and the carpet on the stairs has worn right through. It's also cold in here. Much colder than outside.

"Hello!" I echo. "Hello!"

Florence tiptoes through the hall to the room at the back while I hesitate by the door that must lead to the front room.

I tap gently with my knuckles but in my heart I know that no one's going to answer me. For a moment I close my eyes and breathe. I don't want to do this. I really don't want to do this. "Hello!" The word escapes my teeth far too brightly, and I panic and push the door open. It swings easily and then thumps into the wall behind. From here, I can see the sofa and the chair and a vase of dead flowers.

"Is there anyone here?" I ask, stepping in to the room and looking straight ahead. Drops of water thump on the windowsill outside, but otherwise it's silent. Too silent. Eventually I let my gaze fall to the floor.

It's a body. A man. Dressed in cargo pants, green jacket, boots – earth and mud all over them – and his eyes staring straight at me. I stare back.

"What is it?" says Florence, crashing into the room. "What have you— Oh!" She stops.

A silent minute passes.

"Is he dead?" she whispers.

I nod.

"I've never seen a dead person," she says.

We both stand still, looking down at him. His arm is raised above his head, lying across his ear, his other arm stretched out in front of him, fingers around the shaft of a spade. My first thought is that he's brought a lot of mud into Laura's house. Second — why would he need a spade in here? The floor's solid, no one could actually dig through it.

Not moving any closer, I examine the blade of the spade. It has a dark stain on it, which doesn't look like earth, and he, the man on the floor, has a long gash down the top of his head. They match.

"Police," says Florence.

"Yup," I say, trying to sound glib. "They're gonna love this."

Chapter 22

She calls the police from her phone. I'm surprised they haven't blocked her number.

"Yes, we've found a body."

She walks round the figure lying on the ground. She's so much braver than me. I can't quite bring myself to get any closer. "Man – sixty? Seventy? I don't know. Yes, I'm not an idiot, definitely dead. One thousand per cent dead."

She wanders back out of the room and I follow. I do not want to be in the room alone with him. Not at all, so while she talks to the police, I poke around the rest of the house, nosing into each cupboard and doorway, not sure what I'm looking for, just looking.

"No – no sign of anyone else here…" says Florence, glancing up the stairs and shrugging. I pull her towards the doorway. We should be outside.

Florence's listening and nodding and shrugging and I feel more and more nervous. And I'm beginning to think over the thing I was thinking earlier. So if the man lying on the floor is Thomas Fear, and the woman in the hospital is Laura Fear, and the man in the lake is Derek Fear, then that leaves Sarah Fear. Who could she be? She'd be at least sixty, wouldn't she? And if Thomas Fear dug up the gold, then what did he do with it? It's not here. And who even knew he was doing it?

Florence's babbling down the phone and I'm putting the puzzle together, piece by piece, ruling people out, until I'm sure.

There is only one person who knew about Thomas digging in the graveyard. One person who knew about us poking around. One farmer. One person with a tractor. Who would have had access to our house.

I pull on Florence's sleeve, dragging her away. She resists, still talking to someone at the other end.

"Florence – we have to get to Mum." Florence frowns, but stabs at her phone while telling the person at the other end, "Gotta go."

I don't stop to explain, but run out of the garden into the road, racing uphill past the other cottages on to a patch of green and skirting up towards the dam. My head is buzzing but I know that I have to get to Mum. She's not safe and I reckon that if I go this way, past the reservoir, we might just gain a minute. Florence trots behind me, her boots whomping with every stride. "What's happened?" she shouts.

"Cat," I yell as I run up the long grassy slope that comes out of the top of the village.

"What about her?"

"She's Sarah Fear's daughter – she has to be. She has to be the only remaining member of the family." We're stumbling up the slope, out of breath. "She said she came here to visit relatives. When she was little – in nineteen seventy-six. She was here then, she said it when we were in the pub. And she was probably here to bury her granddad. Remember?"

We run side by side, slipping on the wet grass.

"You're right. So do you think she knew where the gold was all this time, or did you just tell her?"

But I don't answer. We've reached the side of the dam and I almost don't recognise it. Everything's changed since yesterday. Below us to the left is the village, in front of us the reservoir has become a brown boiling thing fed by millions of tiny brown streams flowing from the fields. The car's almost back under the water and all but the top of the gazebo; Mum's dig has totally vanished. How could it fill up so fast? It's much bigger than I thought it could be. It looks as if it could burst at any second.

Below us, emerging from sluice gates at the bottom of the dam, the actual river is seething and dark, swollen from all the rainwater. A small branch bobs up in the flow, circling and bashing at the sides before bouncing on downstream.

Two men in high-vis jackets are standing on the top of the dam looking worried as all along the rim of the reservoir new gullies are appearing and the earth that held them back washes into the water. Small rivers are now shooting from the rim down into the lake and I can see exactly how the reservoir's filled up so fast. The men on the side lower a measure and shake their heads at the result, but surely all those bags of cement must be holding the dam back.

The men shout something to us as we head towards the steps.

"Keep back, don't——"

I point down the steps. That's where our cottage is. That's where Mum is.

The Land Rover is parked outside the cottage.

That's where Cat is.

Then there's a boom as a small chunk of the dam wall breaks and thunders down to the river below.

The men stare and I run, falling over my feet, grabbing the hand rail, watching as a waterfall suddenly appears at the top of the huge bank that holds the water back from the village. Most of the water is hitting the river, but some of it's hitting the road alongside, sweeping it away. Cat's Land Rover sinks as the road surface disappears.

Florence shouts something behind me, but I can't stop. I have to get to Mum. Just as I reach the bottom step, the water cuts through the ground, dislodging tarmac and stone and leaving the huge tree next to the cottage rootless and wobbly. It trembles as another chunk of dam pops out and a new shoot of water bashes into the trunk. The tree sways, pirouetting mid-fall, then speeds and crashes on to the cottage. Roof tiles ping through the air, smashing into the stream below, and suddenly the cottage is on an island surrounded by fast-flowing water.

"Mum!" I shout, picking my way to the side of the stream. Florence is at my elbow, yelling something in my ear about branches.

"We need to make a bridge!" she cries.

She's right. So much rubbish has come through and over the top, the debris is forming a small dam. It just needs a little help. Florence is already pulling at a branch. I grip the other end and we lug it to the narrowest point. Together we build the worst bridge ever, but I don't care, and run on to it slipping and sliding and grabbing at the air until I land by the cottage. Florence skims over the dam, just as a siren goes off.

"Evacuation!" she yells.

I run for the front door. The water's already up

to my ankles.

"Mum!" I shout. "Mum!"

I turn, stumbling, falling into the icy water and a figure appears in front of me. It's Cat. Her hair's hanging over her face and she looks wild. Angry. Dangerous. She's got a huge wheely suitcase. And she's blocking the door to the sitting room.

"Get out, Cat. The dam – it's collapsing," I say, standing. "We have to get out. Where's Mum?"

I push the kitchen door open. Mum's standing there staring at the floor.

"What's going on, Dan? Where's all this water from?"

Behind me I hear laughter, and the kitchen door slams with us inside.

"Cat! Cat!" I shout, whipping round to throw my weight against the door but it won't budge.

"Cat?" says Mum, panic rising in her voice as the water rises around her shins. "What's happening? I don't understand."

"I have to get out," shouts Cat from the other side of the door. "I'm sorry, but you're going to have to stay here until I'm out of the way. Thanks for your help moving it all, Rachel!"

"What's she talking—"

"Bye!" yells Cat.

"No!" I bash on the door and Mum joins me, both of us slapping and banging and shouting but all I can hear is the roar of water, and the door's rock solid. Cat's jammed something against it.

"Mum, what did you help her move?" I clamber on to the kitchen worktop to see out of the window. Cat's made it to the Land Rover, but the water's already deep around the sides and for some reason it's not moving.

"Boxes. Heavy boxes. She had a load of heavy boxes in a shed in the village and we put them in the Land Rover. But I still don't get it. Why did she shut us in? Help! Help!" shouts Mum. "Help. Someone!"

I try to open the kitchen window, but it's one of those stupid safety ones that only opens about three centimetres. Then I try kicking it. It won't give. It's too solid.

A chunk of masonry crashes down outside the window. The house is collapsing.

"If we don't drown, we'll be crushed to death," says Mum. "There has to be a way out." She joins me and both of us struggle to kick in the window that won't break.

"Dan?" comes a voice from the other side of the door. "Dan?"

"Florence! Can you open this door?"

"No," she shouts. "There's a piece of wood jammed against it, and it's..." She groans; she must be trying to move it. "...too heavy. Hopeless."

"It's Cat, Florence – you've got to stop her!"

"S'all right – I have."

"What on earth?" asks Mum.

"How?"

"Water in her petrol tank."

"Genius! But we have to get out of here!"

"Find another way – not the door! Oh no, she's coming back!" yells Florence, and I hear her feet on the stairs. Then there's shouting, Cat screaming at Florence and something thumps overhead.

I start tearing open the kitchen cupboards. "There must be something in here we can use."

More thumps and a scream come from overhead, and then someone runs down the stairs. I hope it's Florence.

"A screwdriver. Find a screwdriver!" I'm

wrenching the drawers out, chucking them on to the countertop; there's got to be something.

The thumping goes on overhead, then there's a crash and a load of tiles cascade down past the windows.

"Screwdriver – here!" shouts Mum. "Two!"

"Windows, undo those catches!" I say, and we both scrabble on to the worktop and struggle with the metal bars holding the windows closed.

"No!" Mum shouts as her screwdriver skids over the metal restraining rod and shoots out into the garden water.

I pause. I must not panic. Holding the screwdriver in both hands I slot it into the screws. It's too big and slides around, but slowly, each time I try, the screw rises a little from the hole until it pings out. Now the second one. Again, pausing for breath, I turn the screw, a tiny bit at a time and it falls so that the window is suddenly swinging free.

"Jump! Go!" shouts Mum.

A moment later I'm outside the house. Above me the dam is bulging, pinging stone blocks down towards the cottage. A man with a hard hat is shouting something from the steps at the side but there's a river that's appeared between us and I can't hear him and I'm honestly too worried about Florence to hang around trying to listen.

"Florence!" I shout up at the cottage. The roof has caved in completely, the branches of the tree filling the space where the roof should be. And it's become an island in the middle of a huge, wide, angry brown river.

"Here!" shouts Florence, appearing from the branches and clambering down a pile of rubble that's propping up the side of the building. "Here!"

"Where's Cat?"

She points towards the river that's pouring into the village.

In the middle, Cat's struggling with the suitcase she had before. I'm guessing it's full of the gold. The water is up to her thighs and she's wading through it, dragging the suitcase, but it's so heavy she's barely moving.

The man in the hard hat's found a long ladder and he's laid it over the gap to the cottage.

"Dan!" Mum points at him and, wobbling over the piles of debris, reaches the end of the ladder. "Dan!" she shouts again. The man leans forward, steadying the ladder, and she begins to cross, but I glance towards Cat.

I can't let her get away.

"We have to stop her!" yells Florence, crashing through the rubble and falling almost flat in her attempt to reach me.

She's right. Ignoring Mum's shouts, I turn and wade into the water. It's icy, and the current whisks my feet away with every step, but Cat's fighting an enormous suitcase full of gold and that has to be harder.

Behind me Florence's splashing and swearing and crashing, and then soon she catches up and overtakes.

"We gotta stop her, Dan," she pants. "She'll be out in a moment on the road. She'll get away."

We race together, fighting the waist-deep water, battling the uneven ground, the potholes that have appeared in the tarmac. I step and fall up to my neck; Florence reaches out her arm and pulls me up. "Keep going!" she says.

Ahead of us, Cat's almost on to solid ground. I glance round. Mum's cleared the ladder bridge and she and the high-vis man are looking up at the dam. Mum's mouth is open and the man lifts his arm to protect his face. And then I realise I can hear a rumble, an awful deep rumble, and above me there's a cloud of spray and dust. That's what they're looking at. In that moment the dam collapses. Stone spills out towards us, chased by a wall of water.

"Dan!" shouts Mum.

"Florence!" I yell.

It hits me, smothers me, whisks me up and down, knocking me off my feet, sucking the air from my lungs. For a second I think I'm probably already dead, and then I bump into something hard and struggle up. It's a wall. A garden wall. Florence shoots past me, and I'm seized by the water, bounced on, desperately reaching for branches and bashing into underwater obstructions. I go under, bob up and go under again, before being dragged to the surface. It's Florence, clinging to a fence post, and she's pulling me up.

"Dan! Don't drown!" she shouts, yanking the front of my T-shirt, but I'm sucked back into the muddy water.

Fighting for the surface I try to thrash out for

the side. Mum and the high-vis man are shouting and I try to get towards them, but the current has other ideas, sweeping me away to the side, until I crash into Cat who is stationary in the middle of the flow, hanging on to something under the surface.

What?

Oh, I know, the stupid suitcase.

"Let it go!" I shout.

"No!" she yells back.

"You gotta let go, you're going to drown!"

From the corner of my eye I see that Florence has somehow swum to the side. She's beached, and Mum and two men are pulling her out. I glance back towards the cottage. Two huge roof beams are being tugged by the stream. Any second now they're going to break away and be swept towards us. Above the cottage, where the dam has broken, a vast green waterfall is beating on its remains, smashing everything below it. The island has completely disappeared. We're only being held here by the weight of the gold. But we can't stay. We'll be crushed, or drowned, or both.

"Cat — please — let go!" I say, both of us still

gripping the top of the case.

"I've waited my whole life," she says, her face wet and wild, with tears or the flood I don't know.

Mum's screaming at me from the bank. The two men, Mum and Florence are pushing the ladder out towards us. It's almost close enough to grab if I could just get past the brushwood that's jammed on something under the surface. I launch myself into the flow and my fingertips reach the end of the ladder.

"Yay!" shouts Florence from the bank as the four of them brace and stop me from bashing into another low wall.

"Come on," I say, latching the fingers of my left hand round the last rung and extending my arm towards Cat.

"Leave me," says Cat.

"No!" I say. "I can't."

"Dan – you don't give up, do you?" she says, letting go of the suitcase and immediately drifting downstream.

"NO!" I shout, kicking up with my legs, hooking her under her arm and tugging against the river.

"Hang on!" shouts Florence. "Hang on!"

As they begin to haul the ladder back to the bank, dragging us over the debris and through the brown boiling water, I reach out again with my right arm and grip Cat's collar. I am not going to let go.

Agonisingly slowly we thump into the side, beaching on the gravelly path.

One of the men from the dam pulls Cat out over me and newt-like I crawl from the mud to sit, soaked, on the side.

No one speaks; we all stare as the wall of the cottage collapses, another wall follows and the roof beams are swept downstream.

"Whoa," says Florence.

I nod. I really can't speak.

A third man in a high-vis jacket runs down from the top and looks at us.

"Is there anybody in there?" he says, pointing at the remains of the cottage.

Mum shakes her head, and tries to speak.

"We're all here," says Florence. "We're fine."

Chapter 23

They take Cat away in a black van.

Not that the police really believe me, although DS Patel, who had come to see the car that day, does narrow her eyes at me as if she thinks there's something in my story.

"And the body's in Mrs Fear's house?"

So tired I can hardly keep my eyes open, I agree that it is, although Florence, filled with some kind of superhuman energy, is able to explain all of it, several times, to each police officer in turn, and to Mum and to her granddad.

"Cat was Sarah Fear's daughter and she married a local farmer so that she could come back here and search for the gold," says Uncle Tony, gazing into the middle distance. "Yup, that figures."

We're sitting in the pub now. It's a little higher than the rest of the village, and, according to engineers, not in danger of flooding. The deluge that swept away the cottage has taken two houses, the scaffolding on the village hall and several gardens, but it's also reduced the likelihood of everything else being destroyed. The village is a total mess, and full of emergency crews, but nobody was killed. Which is incredible when you think about it.

The rain's stopped and now it's all steaming, but we're safe in the snug, eating chips. Mum just keeps on saying "Oh, Dan. Oh, Dan" over and over. I'd happily curl up alongside her and sleep if I could, but people keep on coming to talk to us, and looking at us and saying things like "You were lucky" and "What are the chances of that?"

Florence's granddad is still trying to figure it all out. "Sarah Fear, have to say I don't remember her. She must have told her daughter about the gold, but neither of them ever knew where it was. I don't expect poor old Laura Barlow had a clue, and Thomas just waited all these years to get it."

"Where's it now?" asks Tony.

Mum sighs. "The stuff that's not in the suitcase is in the Land Rover."

"Seriously?"

I flump back against the cushioned pew and dip a chip slowly into ketchup.

We sit in silence and then the same tired policeman who we've seen so many times comes in and sits down in front of me. He takes one of my chips, scoops up the ketchup and stuffs the chip in his mouth.

"Hello," I say.

"Hello, Daniel." He nods towards Florence. "Florence, all of you. I think we may owe you an apology."

"Oh?"

The policeman picks chip from his teeth. I notice that for once he's not dripping sweat, although he looks very uncomfortable.

"We've taken Catherine Fowler into custody. She's confessed to moving the body from the car and introducing crows into your house to scare you away. And to the incident with the silage bales, and to putting a swarm of bees inside your car bonnet."

"I thought she was my friend," says Mum quietly.

"She's also confessed to the attempted murder of Laura Barlow and the killing of her uncle, Thomas Fear, in her aunt's house. Although she's claiming self-defence for that one. And she's confessed to hiding a large amount of stolen bullion."

Mum shudders.

"And all this happening here under our very noses, eh, Tony?" says Florence's granddad.

"I know," Tony replies, shaking his head. "Shocking, isn't it?"

Chapter 24

I sleep.

I sleep all day in a bed that Florence's granddad puts in a dusty attic room above the pub.

In my dreams Mum comes to visit, whispers things and slips away. From time to time she holds my hand and I really try to come out of the sleep but I can't and it's only when the sun breaks through and floods the room with yellow light in the evening that I can bear to pull myself into the day.

I wander downstairs to Florence's room, where

she's sitting on her bed examining hairstyles on her phone.

When I step into the room she leaps up and runs towards me, throwing her arms round my neck and giving me the most rib-crushing hug of my life. An age later she lets me go and goes back to sit on the bed.

"Thank you for saving my life," I say in the end.

"*De nada*," she says, laughing. "Emma doesn't believe I did."

"Doesn't matter," I say. "It happened. I seriously owe you."

Florence rolls her eyes. "Just glad you're alive."

I'm saved from saying anything embarrassing by Uncle Tony calling up the stairs. "Kids, can you come down? There's someone here to see you."

Florence jumps to the ground and I follow her down the dark, narrow staircase to the pub below. Mum's handing a cup of tea to a man in a suit with a briefcase who looks utterly out of place in the crumby cosy surroundings of horse brasses and moth-eaten carpets.

He doesn't look like a policeman.

"Good afternoon. I represent an insurance

company. Many years ago, we insured the bullion that was stored at Heathrow Airport. We estimated it at a value of three and a half million dollars at the time, and unfortunately we had to pay that money out to the owner of the gold, a Swiss bank."

"OK?" says Florence. "So?"

"That was nineteen seventy-eight. However, things have changed. Thanks to you, we have recovered fifty-nine ingots and they are worth very much more than they were in nineteen seventy-six. They're actually worth nearer fifty-three million dollars in the current market."

"What!" Florence squeaks.

"Anyway, there was a reward. Back in nineteen seventy-six it was ten thousand pounds, which at that time was a great deal of money. However, so many years have elapsed we think we'd like to increase the reward to two hundred thousand pounds. We'd like you two – Florence, Daniel – to get that reward."

"What?" I say. "What did you say?"

"That's a hundred thousand each!" Florence stares at the wall, mouthing something. "A hundred thousand pounds," I hear her whisper. "I could—"

"Allow me to correct you, young lady," says the man. "Two hundred thousand each."

Mum pours tea over her feet but she doesn't move except to let her mouth fall open.

"But they're only kids," says Uncle Tony.

"Each?" Florence's squeak is practically stratospheric.

The man reaches into his briefcase and pulls out two envelopes. He hands one to Mum and one to Uncle Tony.

"Hey," says Florence, grabbing the two envelopes, glancing at them and handing one to me. "That's our money," she says, scowling at him.

He raises an eyebrow, gives Florence a respectful nod, and from the doorway says, "Don't spend it all at once." A second later he's gone.

Of course, Mum insisted on paying the money into the bank straightaway. I'd have enjoyed looking at the cheque for a few days. There were a lot of noughts. I knew I'd never see anything like it again and I wanted to enjoy it, just as a thing. As an idea.

Gold that I never really saw, turned into noughts. Unreal.

But after we'd paid it in, it became a number on a screen. A big number.

A few days after that, I took some of it out and gave it to the Sandford Village Hall restoration fund. I rang Florence and explained what I'd done.

"You're right," she said. "You're absolutely totally right. I'll do the same thing even if it breaks my heart."

Also, I bought the most expensive bunch of flowers I could get and gave them to Mum.

And when she came back from hospital we bought flowers for Laura Barlow Fear, who stared at us for the longest time before leaning forward and planting slow kisses on each of our foreheads. She didn't say anything else. She didn't need to.

I walked back in silence with Florence and Squish. Butterflies danced in the road. Distantly a dog was barking and a young family of blue tits played through the yew trees, scooping up insects, dive-bombing the graves.

The sun beat down on my head and an unseen breeze scuttled a leaf along the road.

"Fancy a swim?" said Florence.